"Nicole, I'm going to put my hands on you."

Ty could still see wariness in her jaded eyes as she turned to look at him.

"You already have, Ty."

"I'm going to put more hands on you." He edged closer to her.

"Why are you announcing this?" He noted that she didn't move away, so he moved closer again.

"So that you don't kick my ego into next week, my warrior princess." Cupping her face, he tilted it up. Slowly. Giving her plenty of time to settle in. Or back away.

She didn't back away.

"I'm going to kiss you now. Say yes."

"Ty—"

"Yes or no, Nicole." He looked deep in her eyes, waiting for her answer.

"Yes. Okay? Yes! Put your hands on me." Her arms snaked around his neck, her hands fisted in his hair. "Kiss it all away. Can you do that?"

"Oh, yeah." His hands slid from her face to her hips and he pulled her close. "I can definitely do that."

Dear Reader,

We're back to South Village for Nicole's adventure into love. Adventure? Maybe I should say her *fall* straight into love. The genius Dr. Nicole Mann doesn't take to anything that doesn't involve work. Dedicated to her profession and little else, she's what you might call a one-track woman.

That is, until Ty comes along and distracts her with a sexy Irish lilt and a smile that does something funny to her insides. I hope you enjoy her fall!

And next month be sure to catch my third book in the SOUTH VILLAGE SINGLES series, *Messing With Mac*, where we'll see if the last of these three friends can hold on to her vow of singlehood.

I wish you all happy reading!

Jill Shalvis

P.S. I love to hear from readers! You can reach me through my Web site, www.jillshalvis.com, or by writing me at P.O. Box 3945, Truckee, CA 96160-3945.

Books by Jill Shalvis

Jill Shalvis
TANGLING WITH TY

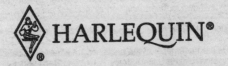

HARLEQUIN®

TORONTO • NEW YORK • LONDON
AMSTERDAM • PARIS • SYDNEY • HAMBURG
STOCKHOLM • ATHENS • TOKYO • MILAN • MADRID
PRAGUE • WARSAW • BUDAPEST • AUCKLAND

To Megan Nicole, my warrior princess

ISBN 0-373-69114-9

TANGLING WITH TY

Copyright © 2003 by Jill Shalvis.

1

A NAKED MAN would have changed everything, but there wasn't one in sight. So, as always, Nicole Mann got up with the alarm. As always, she showered, dressed and nuked a breakfast burrito in less than eight minutes.

And as always, she was out the door of her apartment at top speed to get to the hospital for what was likely to be a double shift due to a late-spring flu outbreak.

Yes, her life was completely dictated by her work. So what? Being a doctor was a dream-come-true, and if she'd worked at that dream-come-true nearly every waking moment, forsaking just about everything else—including naked men—she could live with that. Being a doctor was what she'd wanted since she'd graduated high school fifteen years ago at the perfectly extraordinary age of twelve.

"Psst."

For a woman who prided herself on nerves of steel, Nicole nearly leapt out of her skin at the unexpected whisper coming out of the darkened hallway of her apartment building.

But it wasn't the boogey man or any other menacing threat. It was just the owner of the building and her friend, Taylor Wellington, peeking out her door. Taylor was nice and beautiful—reason enough to hate her—but she also happened to be in possession of that disarming ability to talk until Nicole's eyes crossed. It completely wore down her defenses.

That they'd—polar opposites—become friends still baffled Nicole.

"Psst!"

"I see you," Nicole said. "Did I wake you?" Not that the perfectly-put-together Taylor looked anything other than...well, perfectly put together, but it did happen to be the crack of dawn. A time she considered sacrilegious.

"Oh, no, the living dead couldn't wake me," Taylor assured her. "I set my alarm so I'd catch you." Her beautifully made-up eyes toured Nicole. "Honey, I thought we talked about the camouflage gear."

Nicole looked down at her camouflage cargo pants and green tank top, fitting snug to her lean form. Her wardrobe had been formed back in the expensive days of medical school when she'd been forced to shop in thrift stores, but sue her, she'd developed a fondness for the comfortable garb. That Taylor cared what she wore at all was still a surprise.

Nicole had only lived in this South Village building a few weeks, having moved from another larger building where no one ever even looked at one another. She'd only moved because that place had been sold and the new owners had plans for it to go co-op. She'd come here for its convenience to the hospital, and because it was small. Fewer people to deal with. That this building was also falling off its axis was neither here nor there, as Nicole didn't care what it looked like, as long as her bed was in it. "Why did you want to catch me?"

"I knew if I didn't, you'd forget. We're planning Suzanne's engagement party tonight."

Ah, hell. Suzanne Carter lived in the apartment next to Taylor's. The three of them, the only ones in the building, had shared many laughs and much ice cream, but Nicole still didn't want to plan a party where she'd have to dress up and smile and make nice. She hated making nice.

"You'd forgotten," Taylor said.

"No, I..." Okay, she'd forgotten. She couldn't help it, she was single-minded. Always had been, just ask the family she never managed to see. This year alone, she'd forgotten one sister's homecoming from college, her mother's annual April Fool's Day bash and her own birthday. But her family understood something Taylor didn't.

Nicole was a firm loner. Connections to people tended to give her hives. Ditto planning engagement parties. "I'm sorry. I...might be late."

Taylor gave her a long look. "Don't tell me. You have something new to pierce."

Nicole rolled her eyes. Taylor had been teasing her about the silver hoops she had lining one ear, but Taylor had no way of knowing that each was a trophy of sort, and a badge of honor worn proudly. "Not a new piercing, no."

With the patience of a saint, Taylor just lifted a brow.

Nicole racked her brain for her elusive people skills, but as she didn't have any, they failed her. "We're short-staffed at the hospital, and—"

"Save it, Super Girl." Taylor lifted a hand against the upcoming stream of excuses. "Let's just cut to the chase, shall we? Weddings, and all the trappings, give both of us gas." She looked right into Nicole's eyes and gave her a take-your-medicine look. "But this is for Suzanne."

Suzanne had been the only other person besides Taylor to instantly, genuinely accept Nicole, no matter how abrupt, aloof and self-absorbed she was.

The three of them had only met recently after Taylor had inherited this building with no funds to go with it. She'd rented out space to Suzanne first, then Nicole had come along. They had little in common really. Suzanne, a caterer, kept them in to-die-for food and Suzanne's personal favorite, ice cream. Taylor, with her dry wit, kept them all amused and, though she'd kill Nicole if she heard her say it, mothered them to death. And Nicole...she had no clue what she added to the mix, so them caring about her still mystified.

But they all shared one common trait—a vow of singlehood. They'd talked about it, often toasted to it and had jointly coveted it... Until Suzanne had done the unthinkable and fallen in love.

Nicole sighed. "I'll find a way to be here."

"Don't worry, they say you can't catch wedding fever."

"Hey, don't worry about me. My work is my life. I'm too into it, too selfish to be anything but single."

"Right. Our singlehood is firmly intact."

"Firmly."

But they stared at each other, a little unnerved. That Suzanne, one so steadfastly single, was now getting married cast a shadow on their vow. Surely neither of them could possibly make the fall into love. Not when they kept their eyes open and their hearts closed.

Yep, heart firmly closed. They were safe that way, totally and completely safe.

TWENTY-FOUR exhausting hours later, again just before dawn, Nicole dragged her sorry, aching body back up the three flights of stairs to her loft apartment.

It was dark again, or still. It seemed she lived in the dark.

Work had been especially brutal. An unexpected heavy fog had created a pile-up on Highway 5 South. As a result of the forty-two car accident, she'd been in emergency surgery all day, without a break to so much as sneeze. She'd removed two spleens, pinned four legs, reset more shattered ribs than she could remember, and had delivered twins in an emergency caesarian.

Then she'd been asked to stay another shift, and after a quick nap when she'd dreamed of being chased by a white wedding dress and cake—where had *that* come from?—she'd willingly taken on whatever had come her way. And plenty had.

Now all she wanted was food, a shower and a bed, and not necessarily in that order. She had her Taco Bell bag clutched to her chest, her mouth watering in anticipation of the four regular tacos and extra-large soda. Not the usual breakfast of champions, but food was food and she'd been craving spicy since her second surgery.

And then after the food…oblivion. At least until she had to be back at the hospital again, which happened to be that afternoon for a staff meeting, and then to cover someone else's shift that night. She already had four surgeries lined up, ready to go.

Had she remembered to grab the hot sauce? She

hoped so, she was pretty certain her kitchen—if you could call the hole in the wall that—didn't have any food in it except for something that had gone green a week ago, and—

"You little buggering piece of sh—" A rustling sound, followed by the squeal of metal on metal, blocked out the rest of that shocking statement made in a deep, Irish brogue. "I'm going to...damn me again, you worked at the last job, so bloody hell if you won't work here..."

This was spoken so calmly, so confidently in that accent, it took a moment to decipher that the man was making some sort of threat.

Fine. Nicole was in the mood to kick some ass, as long as her Taco Bell didn't get crushed. Once in a while, having an IQ higher than her weight had some benefits. During med school she'd needed an outlet for all the technical work so she'd taken karate. Like everything she set her mind to, she'd excelled.

Bring it on. She took a defensive stance, then dropped it to set her food down on the top step. No need to risk breakfast. She moved up the last step. There was nothing on this level but her loft and the attic. Nothing but the narrow hallway, which at the moment had a man lying full-length in it. His arms were outstretched, and he held some sort of measuring tool along the scarred wooden planks, swearing the air blue in the most interesting of Irish lilts.

Nicole had to laugh. Or she would have, if she could have taken her eyes off that long, lean, hard male body stretched out so enticingly on the floor in front of her. He had legs from here to Timbuktu, covered in Levi's that most effectively accented the muscles in his thighs and calves.

And then there was his butt, which was very lovingly cupped in that worn denim. His shirt had ridden up, showing a good amount of tanned, damp skin stretched taut over the rippling sinew of his lower back. The rest of it wasn't bad either, smooth and sleek in the plain light-blue T-shirt that invited her to Bite Me in bold black letters.

In spite of the scare he'd given her, she grinned. Bite Me was her official motto. "Um...excuse me."

His arms, stretched over his head, didn't drop the strange gadget in his hands, which was sending out red lighted bleeps. In fact he didn't do anything but sigh. "Be a luv," he said in a voice deep and husky as sin but suddenly utterly devoid of the accent. "And hand me my notes?"

Nicole, still in her defensive stance, craned her neck and saw a small notepad at his hip. It looked as if it had been roughly stuffed in and out of a pocket on a regular basis.

Apparently she hesitated a hair too long, because he pushed up to his elbows and turned his head, giving her a glimpse of jet-black hair cut so short it stuck up in spikes, hitting her with the lightest, most crystal-clear blue eyes she'd ever seen.

He took one look at her with her fists still up, her legs slightly bent and let out another sigh, rubbing his jaw. "We going to duke it out over a notepad then?"

She dropped her fists to her sides, and, keeping her eyes on the most gorgeous stranger she'd ever seen, she bent for her Taco Bell bag. "Who are you and why were you swearing in my hallway?"

"Heard that, did you?" He flashed a grin. "I don't suppose you'd not repeat any of it to the owner? She specifically said no swearing in her hallways."

Hmm. Nicole was surprised Taylor hadn't put this man under lock and key in her bedroom, given her fondness for horizontal gymnastics, and the fact that sexuality rolled off this man in waves.

With one smooth motion, he came to his feet, startling her anew because, granted, she was on the shrimpy side of average height, but he and his hard-as-granite body had to top six feet by several inches.

Which meant her head, if she lifted her nose to nosebleed height, maybe came to his broad shoulder. Between their height discrepancy and her sudden, startling attraction to him, she felt defensive. She hated feeling defensive. It tended to put her on the offensive. Taking one step back, she balanced her weight on the balls of her feet, once again ready for anything.

"Wouldn't have used that language if I'd have heard you coming." A bit chagrined now, he cocked his head and scratched his jaw, which, judging by the dark shadow there, he hadn't shaved in a few days. "Went and startled you, I see."

She narrowed her eyes. Yep, his accent was gone, but there was something stilted about how he sounded now, as if he were hiding something.

She knew well enough about hiding secrets, but didn't like it when others did the same. "Answer my questions, please."

As she'd raised an accusatory finger directed toward his very fine chest, he lifted his hands in surrender. "No need to shoot, I'm just the architect. Ty Patrick O'Grady at your service."

"You're the...architect."

"For the building here. It's going to be renovated." As if to prove he was harmless—harmless, ha!—he propped up the wall with his shoulder and gave her a disarming little half smile that sent sparks of awareness shivering down her spine. "Needs an architect before anything else, you know," he said. "Turns out this place is a historical monument, and is in desperate need of some serious structural repair."

As the place was smack dab in the middle of elegant, sophisticated South Village, where the rich came to play, and everyone else came to pretend to be rich, Nicole decided she could buy that. Especially since this particular building was the current eyesore of the entire block.

Taylor had been having one expert or another through here for weeks in anticipation of a major renovation. "So you're working up a bid for the owner? Suzanne?" she asked, watching him carefully.

Now he smiled, slow and sure. "No, not Suzanne. *Taylor*, but good try. It'd take more than a peewee to trip me up, darlin'."

A peewee? He'd just called her a peewee? She'd give him peewee.

He lifted one jet-black brow at the narrowing of her eyes, and dared to smile at her obvious temper. "Want to see my ID or are you just going to clobber me with that lovely smelling Taco Bell bag?"

"What happened to your accent?"

His face went curiously blank. "What accent?"

"You had an Irish accent. Are you an immigrant?"

"Yep, just got off the boat from Australia, mate." He grinned. "Or maybe that was..." His accent went from Aussie to Austrian in a heartbeat. "From another continent entirely."

A smart-ass. "It's awfully late to be working on a bid."

"You mean early, don't you?"

That might be; she had no idea whether she was coming or going. "Whichever. Why are you here now?"

"I'm what you'd call a busy man...now, darlin', you've got me so flustered, I've gone and missed your name."

Nicole crossed her arms. "It's not darlin', I'll tell you that."

He let out another smile, which she had to admit could melt bones at fifty paces. "Do I have to guess then?"

"Dr. Mann," she grudgingly gave him. "Now, if you don't mind, I've got tacos to eat." And a date with a bed.

Alone.

Where that thought came from, she had no earthly clue. She always slept alone.

Always.

She stared at him still staring at her with a little, knowing smile that made her want to grind her teeth for some reason. "What? You going to make a crack about me being far too young to be a doctor? I get a lot of little-girl jokes. Go ahead, give me your best shot."

He took a good, long look down her body, then slowly, slowly back up again, stopping at the points that seemed to be connected to her loins, since they all came alive with a little flutter that annoyed her even more. "You look all woman to me."

Oh, definitely, she was too tired for this. She brushed past him and stopped at her door, slapping her myriad of pockets, looking for the keys she could never quite remember where she'd left.

"Problem?"

Scowling, she ignored him and switched her Taco Bell bag to the other arm to check her back pocket. No go. Damn, that was the trouble with cargo pants. Comfortable, yes. Practical, with their twelve million pockets to lose things in, no.

"Dr. Mann—"

"Please," she said to that quiet, outrageously sexy voice as she closed her eyes. "Just...go away." If she didn't gobble the food and hit the bed, she'd fall asleep right here on her feet.

She could do it, too. She'd slept on her feet before, during med school, during the long nights of residency....

A sharp click had her blinking rapidly at her...opened door? Ty Patrick O'Grady, architect, sometimes owner of a sexy Irish lilt, man of a thousand curses and one incredible smile, held up a credit card. "Handy, these things, aren't they now?"

"You...broke in?"

"Easily."

"Are you a criminal?"

He laughed, low and sexily, damn him. "Let's just say I've been around. You need a better lock."

"You can't just—"

"Did you find your keys?"

"No, but—"

"Just get inside, darlin'." He gave her a gentle shove as he took the Taco Bell bag from her fingers just before the thing would have dropped to the ground. "Before you fall down."

She stepped over the threshold, reaching back to slam the door. Unfortunately he was on the wrong side of that door and ended up inside her very small place, which seemed that much smaller with his huge presence in it. "And I'm not your darling," she said, turning away.

"Nope, you're Dr. Mann."

She sighed and faced him again. "Okay, so I'm stuffy when I'm tired. Sue me."

"I'd rather call you by your first name."

"Nicole," she snapped, then grabbed her Taco Bell from his fingers and headed into the kitchen, which happened to be only about four steps in. "Feel free to let yourself out."

Naturally, and because she suspected he was as ornery and contrary as he was magnificent looking, he followed her instead.

"What are you doing?" she demanded.

"Making sure you don't fall down on your feet."

"We've already established I'm a grown-up."

"You're right about that. Um..." He watched her shove aside a pile of medical journals and rip into the bag with a wince. "How about some real breakfast?"

"This *is* real." And her mouth was watering. "Goodbye, Mr. Architect."

"You know, you're very welcome," he said when she grabbed a taco, leaned against the counter and took a huge bite. "Glad I could help."

"Yeah. Thank you for breaking and entering." She nearly moaned when the food hit her tongue, but managed to hold it back, sucking down a good part of her soda before practically inhaling the rest of her first taco.

When she reached into the bag for the next one, he sighed.

She eyed him. "You forget where the front door is? Wouldn't want it to hit you on your way out."

"You should really make yourself some healthier food—"

"There's meat, cheese, lettuce and shell here...I've got all the food groups represented."

"Yes, but—" He watched her lick a drop of sauce off her thumb. "I'm assuming you just got off some brutal shift at the hospital?"

"Yeah..." She paused for a long, amazingly refreshing gulp of soda. "Don't take this personally, okay? But could you go away? I've got a date with my bed, and it doesn't include anyone else but me and my pillow."

"Now that's a crying shame." He added a slow grin that upped her pulse.

"Don't get any ideas. I don't play doctor with strangers."

"Who'd want to play with *that* attitude?" He grinned when she growled at him. "And I wasn't propositioning you, Dr. Nicole Mann. I just think you should eat something that has more nutrients than...say a paper bag. Why don't you let me cook—"

He broke off when she burst into laughter. Feeling less like she was going to die on the spot now that she had something in her belly, she set down her taco and headed for the front door. While she was certain he could "cook" up something all right, she wasn't interested. Yes, she enjoyed looking at a great specimen of a man such as himself, but she didn't feel the need to do more than look. "Goodnight," she said, holding the door open.

"Let me guess..." He sauntered up to her with that loose-hipped stride of his, all long, lean grace. His eyes, those amazing blue, blue eyes, seemed to see straight through her. "You have a thing against real food?"

"No, I have a thing against strangers offering to cook for me. Let's face it, Mr. Architect." She offered him a nasty smile she reserved for the lowest forms of life—men on the prowl. "You weren't offering to cook me *food*."

"I wasn't?" He lifted a black brow so far it nearly

vanished. "And what did you think I *was* offering to cook?"

"Let's just say I'm not interested, whatever it was."

With a slow shake of his head, his mouth curved. He wasn't insulted. Wasn't mad or irate. But he *was* amused at her expense.

"Let's just say," he said, mocking her.

"Goodnight," she repeated, wondering what it was about him that made her both annoyed and yet so...aware.

"Goodnight. Even though it's morning." He lifted a finger, stroking it once over her jaw before turning and walking out the door.

When he was gone, she put her finger to her tingling jaw. It wasn't until a moment later she realized his last few words, "even though it's morning," had been uttered in that same Irish accent he'd claimed not to have.

THAT DAY Ty pulled his own long shift. He had three jobs going in downtown Los Angeles, two in Burbank, four in Glendale and, he hoped, the new one right here in South Village.

It was odd, how fond he'd become of the place. Maybe because the city, just outside of Los Angeles, was a genuinely historical stretch of streets from the great old-Western days. Thanks to an innovative—and wealthy—town council, most of the buildings had been rescued, preserved and restored, leaving the streets a popular fun spot filled with restaurants, theaters, unique boutiques and plenty of celebrities to spy on.

Ty had little interest in the swell of young urban singles that crowded the streets on nights and weekends, but he did love the atmosphere.

He especially loved all the work, for there were plenty of buildings still in the pre-renovation stage, needing architects.

Being a relatively new architect in town without the usual partners and office staff meant more work for him. It meant a lot of running around. It also meant lots of time holed up with his drawing table.

He didn't mind the extra hours or the hard work. In fact, that was how he liked it. If something came easy or was handed to him, he was suspicious of it.

That came from his early years, when nothing had been either easy or handed to him, before or after he'd quite literally crawled, scratched and fought his way out of the gutter.

Old times, he thought, and tossing his pencil down, he leaned back in his chair. He put his feet up on the drawing table and looked out the window at the San Gabriel Mountains. No doubt, California was beautiful. Not beautiful like say...Rio. Or Tokyo. Or any of the many places he'd been through on his quest to get as far away from where he'd started as possible, but beautiful in the way that he felt...at ease.

Not that the feeling would last, it never did. Sooner rather than later the need to move on would overcome him...he thought New York might interest him. But for now, California, land of hot blondes, health food and sandy beaches, was good.

It was also a great place for anonymity, and that, really, was the draw. Here, he could be whoever or whatever he wanted. It didn't matter to anyone.

And here, surrounded by the success he'd so carefully built, he was exactly that.

Someone.

Someone with a full bank account, thank you very much. And an office that spelled success, inside a huge, sprawling house with every luxury at his fingertips.

Never again would he have an empty belly or the bone-gnawing fear of the unknown, both of which he'd lived with during his beyond-humble beginnings in the seediest of areas in Dublin, Ireland.

He rarely thought of it now, there was no need. He'd put it all behind him, years and years ago. He'd moved on.

Now nothing could hurt him as he continued on his merry way to fill the bank account even more, to do the work that so pleased him. And if he managed to get lucky in between those two things with a California babe here and there, so much the better.

He thought of this morning, and one Dr. Nicole Mann. Not the typical California babe, that was certain. But with her fatigues and tough take-it-on-the-chin attitude, she was easily the sexiest little number he'd ever seen. And he did mean little, for she'd barely come to his shoulder. Still her body had been honed to a curvy, mouthwatering perfection by what he suspected was sheer will on her part—it certainly wasn't a result of her diet if her "breakfast" was anything to go on. Definitely, the one thing the good doctor had in spades was will. She could kill with just her eyes, these long-lashed, huge eyes, the gray of a wicked winter storm. Her hair, shiny, dark and cut short to her stubborn chin, made him think of silk.

He would have laughed at the impression she'd made on him, if there was anything funny about it. She was different, and because of it she'd grabbed him on a level he didn't want to be grabbed at. So he wouldn't think about her or her perfect, meant-for-hot-wild-sex mouth.

Straightening, he put his feet firmly on the ground. He liked his feet on the ground. To do that, he had to keep a certain distance from others, and that included sexy Dr. Mann. Spinning in his chair, he propelled himself the few feet to his computer and booted it up.

To clear his head of stormy gray eyes and that kissable frown, he'd work.

His e-mail account opened, showing twenty-eight unread messages. Skimming through, he deleted each as he took care of various work issues.

And it was all work. Except the last one. He didn't recognize the sender's address, but didn't think anything of it until he opened the mail.

Are you Ty Patrick O'Grady of Dublin?

Surging to his feet, he stared at the e-mail. The words were still there. Stuffing his fingers in his hair he turned a slow circle. No one knew where he was from. No one.

But when he bent to look at the screen again, the words hadn't changed.

Are you Ty Patrick O'Grady of Dublin?

Hell, yes, he was. But who wanted to know? And why? There was nothing good about his past. In fact, there was so much bad, his stomach cramped just thinking about it.

He reached toward the keyboard to delete the message, but his finger hovered just over the key.

Who was asking?

No. It didn't matter. None of his past mattered, and

with another low oath and yet another slow spin around the room he came back to his computer. Stared at the message some more.

Then slowly reached out and punched Delete.

2

AFTER TWO straight days of hell at work, Nicole drove home. She could tell it wasn't her usual time to be doing so—the usual time being very, very late or very, very early—because there wasn't a single parking space to be found in all of South Village, much less on the busy street where she lived.

Shops, galleries and restaurants were all hopping with activity, reminding her that everyone else but herself had a life outside of work. But then, she'd decided long ago that medicine *was* her life. All she needed now was a place to park her car. Finally, after circling the block—twice—swearing in a very satisfying manner and even getting flipped off in the process, she got a spot down the street. The walk to the apartment felt good. So did the bag of fresh croissants she purchased at a corner deli. They'd go splendidly with the take-out hamburgers in a bag in her other hand.

Finally, she came to her building. It really was the wince spot of the area, though the turrets, mock balconies and many windows gave the hundred-year-old place its own charm and personality. Albeit a neglected, falling-down kind of charm.

The two storefronts on the ground floor were empty, though Suzanne planned to open a catering shop in one of them. Taylor was doing her best, working on the renovation day and night, gathering bids and selling off some of her antique collection to do it.

There were plants hanging from window boxes in front of the two apartments on the second floor. Taylor's boxes were effortlessly green and flowery, Suzanne's looked a little wilted since she spent most of her time at Ryan's now.

Nicole could have bought her own place. Her mother often hounded her about it. After all, doctors made tons of dough, right?

Ha! She was twenty-seven. Maybe by the time she was forty she'd have half her college loans paid off. Then again, given that she tended to spend her extra time working at clinics for free to ensure that the less fortunate got medical care, maybe not. Didn't matter. Work was who she was, what she did and there wasn't time left over to tend to so much as a single little plant, much less a house of her own.

She liked things that way.

Exhausted, she staggered up the stairs to her loft. It was still light outside, which confused her. She squinted at her living room. How different it looked with sunlight streaming through the big window. On the street below throngs of people were heading toward chic restaurants and cafés. A glance at her watch told her why. It was five in the afternoon. People were meeting for after-work drinks or early dinners. The thought of socializing like that startled her somewhat. When she wasn't pouring herself into work, she truly preferred to spend her time alone.

She wolfed down the fast food first, while reading one of three medical journals on the table in front of her. The hamburger and super-size fries were the perfect accompaniment to the article on a new and innovative artery replacement. Then, with the sun still shining in all the windows, she headed into her bathroom, still reading, nibbling on a croissant as she stripped for a mind-numbingly hot shower.

No one could ever say she couldn't multi-task.

After her steaming shower, she padded naked back into her bedroom, heading directly for the bed, until she glanced at her answering machine, which was blinking.

Damn it, why did she have one of those things again?

Because the hospital administration, tired of not being able to get her when they needed, had insisted. With a sigh, she hit the message button. If it was work, she'd just roll over and die right now.

"Nicole, baby, it's me. Mom," her mother clarified in her cheerful, laughing voice, as if Nicole wouldn't recognize the woman who'd been nagging her all her life. "Are you working too hard? Are you getting any rest? Are you eating right? Are you ever going to call me and put my mind to rest that my baby isn't working herself into an early grave?"

Nicole sank to her bed and ran the towel over her short mop of hair—her idea of styling. Since she'd just called her mother last week, in fact, called every week, she refused to feel guilty.

"Once a week just isn't enough, Nicole," her mother said with her perfectly startling ability to read her daughter's mind. "I want to *hear* you."

Nicole rolled her eyes but a smile escaped anyway.

"Honey, listen. I'm making pot roast on Sunday. Your father called your sisters and everyone is coming—the husbands, the kids, everyone."

Oh, good God. Nicole had three sisters, each of whom had a husband, the requisite minivan, the house in the burbs and at least two kids. The thought of that entire noisy, happy bunch all in one place made Nicole suddenly need another hamburger.

"So, honey, you have to come. We'll expect you by four, and let me warn you, if you don't show, I'll...well, I'll call you every single day for a week."

As Nicole's mother was quite possibly the bossiest, nosiest, most meddling, warm, loving person on the planet, Nicole believed her.

But everyone under one roof? Laughing, talking,

happily arguing sisters, sticky toddlers, drooling babies, stinky diapers... She felt a headache coming on already. She loved her family, she did, but sometimes she felt as if she was an alien, plopped down in the middle of a planet where she didn't belong. They were all so...normal. Something she'd never been. Despite her genius IQ, she couldn't deal with people outside of medicine. It was so difficult for her to get out of her own head, she rarely knew what to say to people and some of the basic niceties escaped her. That her family loved her anyway, even though she was intensely introverted, was a strange and odd miracle she tried not to think about too often.

"So, we'll see you Sunday," her mom said as if it'd been decided. "It'll be fun to be all together."

Fun wasn't quite the word Nicole would have come up with. Maybe she'd have work. Yeah, that was it, she could add a shift and—

"Love you, baby."

Ah, hell. Sunday it was.

Still naked, she plopped on the bed. It only took two pillows over her head and approximately twenty seconds for sleep to conquer her the same way she'd conquered her world.

She dreamed. She would have thought she'd be haunted by the blood of her second surgery that day. A patient had burst an artery and by the time she'd gotten everything under control she'd been standing in a sea of red.

But blessedly she'd left that behind at the hospital. Instead, in dreamland, she was two years old again, and memorizing the book of presidents her parents had kept on the coffee table. For fun, she'd recite them backwards to her hotshot, know-it-all sisters Annie and Emma.

It had been their first inkling that Nicole was going to be different.

The dream shifted and she was six, helping Emma with her seventh-grade algebra.

At twelve, she'd helped Annie with her PSAT testing. *A genius*, were the whispers around her. *Off-the-scale IQ*, they said. *A prodigy.*

At twelve, Nicole should have been into lip gloss, pop bands and boys. Instead she'd been fascinated by science. She operated on frogs. She dissected bugs.

Yet kids her own age remained a mystery to her, a complete mystery.

And now that she was grown up, she was still different. She should have learned to deal with others by now. Learned to be a social creature, well rounded and defined.

But the reality was that she'd rarely dated and had no idea how to do anything but heal. It was what she was. Who she was. A doctor.

Nothing else.

So why did the next dream involve one tall, dark and sexy Irish architect with a killer smile and eyes that made her yearn for something completely out of her reach?

Turning over, she sank back into an exhausted and dreamless slumber.

"WAKE UP, Nicole, you're scaring me."

Nicole snuggled more deeply beneath her covers. "Go away, Mom, I don't have school today."

"I had better not look anything like a woman old enough to be your mother."

Nicole jerked her eyes open, heart pounding. Okay, good, she was home. The sun was shining again, how annoying.

And Taylor sat on her bed, looking as stunningly beautiful and elegant as ever.

With a groan, Nicole shut her eyes again. "I didn't help you with the engagement party plans, right?"

"No, but I forgive you because you're going to re-schedule. I brought you breakfast."

Nicole smelled something delicious. She cracked open an eye and saw a tray filled with mouthwatering food.

"I should tell you—as if you couldn't guess—I didn't cook this. Suzanne's catering a big brunch this morning and made this up for us. You frightened the hell out of me, not answering your door. You never even heard me calling for you like a banshee, and we all know I don't like to sound like a banshee. Who sleeps like that?"

Nicole blinked. "Well..."

"You've overworked yourself again, haven't you? Nicole, honey, that's just plain bad for you."

Nicole closed her eyes, rendered stupid by this display of concern. Maybe if she was really still, Taylor would vanish. A figment of her imagination.

"Not much of a morning person," came an amused male voice from the other side of the room.

If Nicole had thought her heart had raced at the sight of Taylor in her bedroom, it went off the scale now. Even after their very brief encounter, she recognized that slightly Irish voice, she recognized it immediately. And if it brought a series of shivers down her spine that she couldn't attribute to a morning chill, she could shove the reaction aside in favor of temper. "What the hell—"

"Now before you get all pissy at me..." Taylor put a hand over Nicole's chest, pushing her back. "Let me explain."

Nicole could take Taylor down any day of the week. Her workouts, when she could fit them in, guaranteed that.

The only exercise Taylor ever did was lifting and setting down her hairbrush. Oh, and her lipstick.

No, what held Nicole back from wrapping her fingers around Taylor's neck was one tiny little detail.

She slept in the nude.

Which meant that in order to kick Taylor's ass, she'd have to get out of bed.

Naked.

"Why is he in here?" she settled for asking between her teeth while clutching the sheet to her chest.

From his perch holding up her wall, Ty's gaze zoomed in on her—a very blue gaze that was lit with amusement, curiosity and plenty more—and for just a flash in time, she lost her train of thought.

Taylor craned her neck and looked up at the tall, dark, ridiculously gorgeous man. "You've met?"

"You could say that," Nicole said.

"Oh, good, because I'm thinking of hiring him to fix up the building, which apparently is about to fall off its axis. Not," she added quickly, "that you need to worry about it, I'm getting it all fixed pronto."

"Taylor." Nicole rubbed her temples. "The point. Get to the point. *Why is he here?* Specifically, in my bedroom."

"Well, I was standing there in the hallway yelling for you, and beginning to freak out when you didn't answer, when he offered to break in since I didn't have my keys on me. He's not only an excellent architect, he's quite the handyman."

"Let me guess," Nicole said dryly, watching Ty

smile at her from behind Taylor's back. "He got in with a credit card?"

"Why, yes. A handy little trick, don't you think?"

"Hmm." Nicole narrowed her eyes at the ease he displayed standing there in her bedroom. As if he belonged.

But no one, especially a man, belonged in her bedroom, no matter how good he looked in a light-blue chambray shirt shoved up past his forearms, and a pair of jeans that made her hormones stand up and quiver. "Is the credit card trick something you picked up in Ireland?" she asked.

"Why ever would you think that?" he asked innocently.

As if he'd ever been innocent. "Because I hear it in your voice."

"That's the English, luv," he said, pushing lazily away from the wall, coming close enough to peruse the tray from Suzanne. Then, picking up a piece of toast, his gaze tracked over Nicole from head to toe, and back again, making every single atom in her body leap to attention. Sinking his teeth into the bread, he chewed a moment, then licked the butter off his finger with a sucking sound that caused an answering tug in Nicole's nipples for some annoying reason. "Went there for a while," he said.

"Thought it was Scotland."

Leaning in, he put the toast to her lips, pressing until she had no choice but to open and take a bite. "There, too," he said lightly, making her take yet another bite, his thumb stroking across her bottom lip at a dab of misplaced butter. "And also Australia, if you're interested in keeping track."

She felt the touch all the way to her toes and back up, and at all sorts of other interesting spots along the way. It didn't help that her eyes were level with a most erotic spot on his body—the juncture between his thighs—and the intriguing bulge there.

"I had to make sure you were okay," Taylor said, picking up a piece of peach from the tray. "I'm sorry for the invasion, but you've done nothing but work since you moved in here, and you sleep like the dead."

Ty let out another innocent smile. "And you talk to yourself while doing it."

Nicole opened her mouth, but Taylor stuffed the peach into it. At the explosion of sweet nectar in her mouth, she sputtered.

"That was a piece of fruit," Taylor said. "I realize you might not recognize it, given that it's actually one of the important food groups and not purchased from a drive-through."

"Taylor—"

"You're going to kill yourself this way," Taylor said softly, her eyes showing their worry. "It's not right. Promise me you'll eat all of this mountain of food. The eggs, the sausage, the toast, the fruit, every-thing."

Nicole sighed. "I never had a landlord care what I put inside my body before."

Taylor went still, then brushed the crumbs off her hands. "Is that all I am?"

Nicole looked into Taylor's eyes, saw the hurt added to the worry, and flopped back to stare up at the ceiling. "*This* is why I don't socialize."

Taylor stood a little stiffly, when the elegant Taylor was never stiff. "I'm sorry. I'll go. Just make sure Suzanne gets her tray back—"

Nicole reached out and grabbed her wrist. "Look...I'm the sorry one."

"No need."

Nicole sighed at the cool hurt lingering in Taylor's face and tugged on her wrist until she sat back at her side. "I'm an idiot, all right? An idiot who doesn't know how to...have friends."

"So we *are* friends?"

"You know we are. Unless you shove any more fruit down my throat."

"In that case..." Taylor spread her silk skirt carefully and made herself comfortable on the bed before reaching for a piece of toast. "There's enough here to feed an army. Ty, some sausage? Don't be shy, hon, Suzanne is so nervous about her upcoming nuptials that she's overcooking to compensate."

"Taylor," Nicole said in a warning voice that turned into a squeak when Ty suddenly joined them.

On the bed.

His long denim-covered legs brushed hers. There were the covers between them, but given the electric zap she felt at the brush of his warm, hard body, and given the way the current continued to run through her, there weren't enough covers in all of South Village to keep between them.

And then there was how her heart gave a little leap when he turned his head and pierced her with those amazing eyes of his.

Instant lust. She'd heard about it but had never experienced the phenomenon firsthand.

She didn't like it.

Gripping the sheet to her chest for all it was worth, Nicole watched as her two uninvited houseguests helped themselves to the tray of food balancing on her knees.

It was an unreal feeling having Ty's long fingers hover over the plate only inches from her very naked body as he decided on a slice of apple.

It crunched between his white teeth as he looked at her.

Unreal, she decided, and definitely...arousing, if the way her body tingled was any indication. "I...need to get up."

Taylor used the fork to bite into the homemade

hash browns, then moaned. "Oh, these. *These* are to die for. Ty?"

Leaning in, he opened his mouth to the forkful Taylor was offering him.

"Fabulous, right?" Taylor said as he chewed.

He licked his lips, and for an instant, as he looked at Nicole, something hot and dangerous flashed in his eyes. "Oh yeah."

"More?" Taylor asked. "A man your size, who works as hard as you do, needs to keep up his strength."

Still gripping the sheet, Nicole grated her teeth. "I really need to— *Hey!*" she said around the bite of warm hash browns Ty shoved into her mouth. And not too gently either. She had to open quickly and use her tongue to keep from spilling them down her front.

His electric-blue eyes never left hers. She would have opened her mouth and blistered him if she hadn't had it so full of the food. And oh man, the food. Heaven.

Not that she was going to admit it. "I don't eat breakfast," she said, trying not to moan in pleasure as the food started to hit her stomach. "Just—"

"Coffee," Ty finished for her, bending so close his lips almost brushed hers. "We've heard. It's here." She could feel his body heat, the warm breath that caused goose bumps to skitter down her side.

"You're going to give yourself ulcers the way you eat." He tsked. "And you claim to be a doctor."

"Oh, I definitely like you," Taylor said to Ty, who grinned at her. "We can tag-team her. I know you like to move around a lot, but I don't suppose after this job you'd stay on and reprogram my friend here?"

"I *really* have to get up," Nicole said, jaw clenched. "So if you could..." She gestured to the door.

"Go ahead." Ty's eyes were lit with the dare. "Get up."

Nicole thought about how very naked she was under her sheet and gripped it tighter to her chest. She'd never been shy, had never felt anything but comfortable in her own skin. This came from years of no privacy in a tiny house with too many family members, then college dorms, and more recently, the locker area at work, which wasn't much bigger or more private than her bedroom happened to be at the moment. But in front of this man, she suddenly felt...inadequate. He was red-blooded, through and through. She figured she knew his type; big boobs and breeding hips, with lots of hair to drape over his chest, that's what he'd want.

Her virtual opposite.

Not that she cared. She just didn't plan to flaunt her small boobs and small hips anywhere near him.

Then, from across the small bedroom, under a mountain of clothes and more medical journals on a chair, came the unmistakable sound of her beeper going off.

Taylor held out her hand to keep Nicole in bed. "It's your day off."

"I can't just ignore it." But it was a shame she hadn't piled more clothes on top of the beeper before last night. A few more days' worth and no one could have possibly heard the thing go off. "Okay, fun's over. You guys did good, you fed me. Now get lost."

"Nicole," Taylor said sternly, still sitting on the bed. "Do not get that pager."

Nicole turned to Ty, whose daring, smiling gaze had never left hers. "I have to."

"Sure you do, darlin'." He lifted an inviting hand. "Go right ahead, if it's meaning that much to you."

"You have to move first."

Generous to a fault, he scooted down on the bed a tad, giving her enough room to leave the bed if she so desired. "Go on now."

With as much dignity as she could muster, which wasn't much, she grabbed the sheet and held on to it for dear life as she slid from the bed. Standing was a bit tricky, but she wrapped the sheet around her so fast her head nearly spun. Surely no one had gotten a glimpse of anything. Still, she didn't quite dare to look back and catch a peek at Ty's face as she headed, chin thrust high, toward the chair.

She had to shove the medical journals and clothes to the floor to verify, but yep, it was work.

"Don't tell me." Taylor stood up. "You're going in. You're hopeless, you know that?" With a dramatic sigh, she headed toward the door. "But we'll be there, Nicole, if you fall."

"We?"

"Suzanne and I, of course. Ornery as you are, you'll need us to stick by you. So go. Go work yourself to exhaustion again. Enjoy."

"I will, thanks." Half amused at the genuine compassion and worry that she'd seen on Taylor's face, she turned back to face Ty. "Don't let the door get you on the ass on your way out. I'm taking a shower."

"Maybe you'd better take your caffeine with you." He held out a mug of coffee.

"Thanks." Grateful but not about to admit it, Nicole held on to the sheet for dear life and hobbled into the bathroom. She shut the door harder than she should have, and clicked the lock into place with what sounded like a gunshot.

She might have had to wake up with an audience, then eat with one, but hell if she'd shower in front of one, no matter how pretty he was.

Still, the hot steam worked wonders, and she stayed there for a good long time, until the hot water turned warm, then tepid. Finally, she stepped out and sighed.

Damn, she'd been looking forward to a day off.

There was one dry towel left on the rack, which meant she needed to seriously consider the pile of things behind her bedroom door as well as the pile now on her floor, both of which she so lovingly referred to as Laundry Mountain Range. Tucking the towel beneath her armpits, she studied herself impassively in the mirror.

Not bad, she'd give herself that. And though she'd prefer to be taller than so damn short, her bones weren't bad either. Thanks to her workouts, she was a lean, mean, fighting machine.

But breasts would have been nice.

Laughing at herself, she turned away. What would she have done with cleavage? It wasn't as if she had dates lining up.

Still smiling, she opened the door and marched into her bedroom, dropping her towel as she went.

Because she had excellent eyesight, she therefore had a front-and-center view of Ty sitting on her bed, holding a glass of orange juice.

He had a front-and-center view, too. Of her.

The glass slipped from his fingers and fell to the floor in tune with her shriek as she bent down for her towel. *"What are you doing?"*

"I..."

Straightening, she studiously avoided looking into

his face as she refastened the towel. "I thought you left!"

"Yeah, I..."

"You said that already!"

Ty knew that, but he was still flummoxed by the sight of her tight, lean body all dewy and damp from her shower. Standing now, he wasn't reassured by the fact his knees wobbled.

What was wrong with him? She wasn't his usual type, meaning stacked and blond and soft. There was nothing soft about Nicole, not her tough, angular body, not her voice, and most definitely not her eyes.

So why couldn't he stop thinking dirty little thoughts? Or take his eyes off her? "Sorry. I just wanted to be sure you at least drank some juice."

"Can't do that now, can I?" With jerky movements, she tightened the towel even further over her breasts.

Breasts that he now knew were a perfect handful, tipped with tight rose-colored nipples. Somehow he managed to walk to her, lift her chin and look into her furious and...damn it, very embarrassed, eyes. "I'm sorry," he repeated softly.

"Yeah."

He gazed at her grim mouth, and unbidden, his thoughts turned to kissing her until she was soft and pliant, until she sighed and gave herself over to him and the pleasure he could give her. He, Ty Patrick O'Grady, no-good bastard, black-heart. "You should know I'm attracted to you in a way I can't quite seem to get over."

"And yet you've seen me naked. Imagine that."

She didn't believe him. He sucked in a breath and inhaled the scent of her shampoo and ridiculously, his body reacted.

Perfect.

Now all his thinking had taken him to a place he had no business going, not with this woman. She wasn't the type to put up with a man afflicted with a serious sense of wanderlust, a man who never knew when he was going to decide to up and relocate.

Hell, he'd never found *any* woman, on this continent or otherwise, who'd put up with that.

Not that he wanted one to.

"You're beautiful, Nicole," he heard himself say as he stroked a finger over her cheek, her jaw. "So damn beautiful."

It wasn't until he got down the stairs and into his car that he let out the breath he'd been holding and stared off at nothing.

He'd meant what he'd said. He was attracted to her in a way he couldn't get past. And she *was* beautiful, with or without that mouthwatering body and all that creamy, creamy skin exposed. So damned beautiful he ached.

Not a good thing, not a good thing at all.

3

NICOLE WORKED so many hours over the next two days she managed to forget Ty had seen her very naked. At the end of a particularly long, atrocious shift, she stood in front of her locker in the doctor's lounge and realized she actually had the next day off.

Sleep, here she came.

"That was an interesting sigh," said a male voice from behind her. A voice that made her wish she'd gotten out of here five minutes ago.

Dr. Lincoln Watts. Head of Surgery. And ruler of his domain.

Not that she didn't appreciate his skill, because he was truly gifted. But that gift didn't extend to his people skills.

In short, out of the operating room, he was a jerk. The nurses hated him, the aides feared him. The other doctors merely tolerated him, mostly because he ruled over all of them, but also because it was too much trouble to cross him.

Oh, and he had the memory of an elephant.

As the youngest doctor on staff, Nicole had learned

to keep a low profile. She did her job; she did it well. It was all she'd ever wanted.

Even with Dr. Watts staring at her ass. "Can I help you?" she asked politely, turning to look at him so he had to raise his gaze.

He took his time about doing so, and for the first time she was glad she had small, unimpressionable breasts. She wanted to give him as little pleasure as possible.

"Can you help me," he repeated with a little smile as he finally met her gaze. "Why yes, I believe you can."

Damn.

"Come with me to the benefit tomorrow night."

The benefit he referred to was an annual event designed to extricate money from rich patrons and deposit it directly to the hospital's coffers. It put critical funds at the hospital's disposal, as well as provided write-offs for the hospital's patrons. Everyone was happy.

However, it required an evening of stiff smiles for Nicole, who hated dressing up, hated being "on" and hated the forced mingling. This year she'd arranged to be on shift so as to avoid the entire messy affair. "Sorry, I'm working."

"I can rearrange that for you."

At a considerable cost, one she figured would involve him and his bed. "No, thank you. I don't mind missing it."

"I want you to come with me."

And what Dr. Watts wanted, Dr. Watts got. "I'm sorry, Dr. Watts, but that wouldn't be fair to the others."

"Linc."

"Excuse me?"

He traced a finger over her shoulder and she just barely restrained her shudder. "Call me Linc," he said softly. "And I'd consider it a personal favor if you went with me."

Nicole might have mastered calculus by the age of eight but she'd never mastered basic political correctness 101. "I said no."

His eyes darkened, and without another word, he strode off.

Uneasy, Nicole watched him go and wondered if she'd just screwed herself by not screwing the boss.

SHE WENT HOME. On the front steps of the building sat a brass lion, its mouth open wide in a silent roar. Shaking her head, she walked past it. Just inside were a vintage-looking gramophone, an ornately decorated headboard leaning against the wall and a marble clock.

Taylor, the poor little rich girl. She'd inherited this building without any of the money she'd become accustomed to in her spoiled youth, with the exception of the antiques she'd been collecting all her life. She'd been selling off the beloved pieces to cover the costs of bringing the building back to its former glory. *Resourcefulness*. It was one of the things Nicole appreciated most about Taylor, as Nicole had been forced to be resourceful all her life.

A three-foot-high wooden carved bear holding a fish and wearing a grin sat on the first flight of stairs. Along the second flight were stacks of prints. Nicole was staring at one of a bowl of fruit, thinking she was just starving enough to actually eat fruit, when Taylor stuck her head out of her apartment.

Damn. More party plans. "I'm really tired," Nicole said pathetically, figuring Taylor would take pity on her.

Instead Taylor reached out, snagged her wrist and yanked her into her apartment. "We need to talk."

"But—"

"You're tired, yeah, yeah. I know. I figured that much and planned the party without you."

Gratitude filled Nicole, and she felt a little bad about her peevishness. "Thank—"

"Don't thank me yet, Super Girl. You're going to need a dress."

"Oh, no—"

"Oh yes. And know it up front, we're going fancy on this one."

"But—"

"That'll teach you to leave me alone to plan things."

"Well, unplan them."

"No." Taylor leveled her stubborn gaze on Nicole. "Suzanne deserves this."

"Yes, but—"

"*Fancy,*" Taylor said firmly. "As in silk and lace and high heels and makeup and hairdos and everything."

Nicole had faced two life-threatening surgeries that day. She'd faced Dr. Watts. And she'd rather face a fire-breathing dragon on top of all of it than get "fancy." "You're kidding me."

"Honey, I never kid about fashion."

Nicole paled. "Fashion?"

"You and me. At the mall. Your next day off."

Nicole let out a string of curses that had Taylor laughing. "Oh, and since you owe me on planning the party without you, you can pay up right now. I need a little favor."

Nicole thought of her bed and sighed. "Taylor—"

"Don't worry, it's not difficult. I just need you to run to Ty's office and give him these." She dumped a large set of plans into Nicole's arms. "And this." She added a file. "Did you like him?"

"What?"

"Did you like Ty?" Taylor laughed at her expression. "What's not to like, right? He's sexy as hell, and in possession of a body I could just gobble up." She sighed dramatically. "It's too bad we're too much alike. We'd kill each other."

Nicole shook her head. "I'm not going to ask."

"But I'm going to tell. Ty and I, we're fellow wanderlust spirits."

"You've got wanderlust?"

"Through and through, until I came here and found home. But Ty hasn't found his home yet. Fighting our own prospective and warring needs would be like living in a battlefield. Nope, much as I'd like a good, naughty affair—and I'm quite certain Ty can do good and naughty—he's not for me."

Nicole put her hands over her ears—or at least she tried to around all the stuff in her arms—and Taylor laughed again. "Just go. Tell him I'm giving him the job. The address of his office is on the label, and it's only three minutes from here."

Before Nicole could blink, she'd been turned around and shoved out the door. She whirled, but only to hear Taylor's lock click into place. "I'm not doing this," she said through the wood.

"Then come back in and help me pick out napkins and plates and menus for the party."

Nicole stared down at Ty's name and address and felt a peculiar flutter in her belly. Why was it that every time she thought of him her skin went all hot and itchy and her nipples got happy? "This is a bad idea, Taylor."

"Since when are you afraid of anyone, much less a man?" Taylor asked through the door.

Since that man could simply look at her and make her feel things she didn't understand. "I...can't."

"Just drop the plans off, Nicole. You don't have to marry him."

Yeah, Nicole. You don't have to marry him. Somehow that didn't make her feel any better. With a sigh, she headed down the stairs instead of up, and got back into her car.

TY HAD a headache and another e-mail. This was not what he needed after a long day at work. He stood staring at it. He shut his eyes, swore, and stared at it again.

I think you're Ty Patrick O'Grady of Dublin.
I think you were born to Anne Mary Mulligan of Dublin. Please confirm.

Margaret Mary

Why a Margaret Mary would be looking for him was anyone's guess, only none of them were good.

Who was this formal-sounding woman, and why did she care who he was? What did she know of the boy he'd been? And he *had* been a boy when he'd left

Dublin, a young boy who'd never looked back. Why should he? He had nothing to look back for, no roots, nothing. His father had taken himself to an early grave in a drunken brawl when Ty had been a year old. His mother had run a tavern with rooms above it she'd used as an inn when they'd needed the money. Which had been all the time. Ty had been nothing more than a mistake she didn't like to be reminded of.

That had often worked in his favor, as he'd had the freedom to do as he pleased. And since his mother rarely remembered to feed him, much less clothe him, and only begrudgingly gave him a mat to sleep on, the freedom pleased him plenty. He "borrowed" clothes, stole food and ran with a crowd that made the L.A. gang-bangers look friendly.

When he'd turned ten he'd witnessed his first murder. Over a pair of boots. When he'd turned eleven, his mother had sold the inn and moved on.

Without him.

By the time he'd turned sixteen, he'd been beyond redemption. Or so he'd thought. That's when he'd made the mistake of trying to pick the pocket of a vacationing Australian. The man, Seely McGraw, had been a cop, of all things, and instead of dragging Ty off to jail, he'd dragged him home with him. To Australia. Ireland had been happy to see him go.

In Australia, Seely had seen him through the rest of

his school years. Civilized. Humanized. And yet the vagabond within him had survived.

When Seely had died, Ty had given in to his wanderlust, going wherever he wanted, when he wanted. Europe, Asia, Africa. Even South America. Then he'd come here, to the States, and had landed in California.

For the first time in his life, he'd fallen in love with a place. Created a home for himself.

He wondered how long that would last before the wanderlust yearning overcame him again. Given his past, he didn't figure it would be long. But for now he enjoyed himself, occasionally marveling over how far he'd come.

Life was good right here, right now. He had a job he loved, and money with which to do as he pleased when he pleased.

But now someone wanted him to think about his past, where he'd been a son-of-a-bitch Irish runaway.

Rare temper stirring, he hit Reply and typed:

Who wants to know?

No, that would only encourage this, when he wanted nothing more than to forget all about it. But before he could delete it, he heard a knock at the front door, which he'd left open for the pizza he'd ordered. He needed that pizza. "Back here!"

Hopefully they hadn't forgotten the beer this time,

he seemed to be in a mood for it. Standing up, he stared down at the computer one more time, stared at his response, finger still poised to delete...

"Ty?"

Not pizza, but Nicole. Her wide gray eyes stared into his, and in a flash, pure lust sped through his blood.

And between his thighs.

Whether it was the monster headache he had, or the unwanted hunger for this woman, it was a weakness, and he hated weaknesses. He wanted the taste of her mouth, the feel of her body beneath his hands, and given her expression, every bit of his wanting showed on his face.

Her mouth opened, then carefully closed. On instinct, he looked down at himself and realized he hadn't put on a shirt after his shower or fastened his jeans.

Doing that now brought her gaze from the tattoo on his arm right down to an area of his body that seemed to have this hyper-awareness of her. "I thought you were the pizza," he said, the metal-on-metal glide of his zipper seeming extraordinarily loud, echoing between them.

"Uh..." Nicole jerked her head up and stared into his eyes with a blank expression, as if she couldn't remember what she was doing there.

Christ, that was arousing.

And confusing as hell, because this woman, and this woman alone, seemed to be able to mess with his head.

She thrust out a set of plans. "From Taylor." She slapped a file against his chest as well. "You've got the job, Mr. Architect." And she turned away.

"Nicole."

She was careful not to turn back to look at him. "Yes?"

What had he been going to say? Something. Anything. "I...got the job?"

"I just said so, didn't I?"

Ah, his sweet, sweet Nicole. "Well, then. We need to celebrate."

She pivoted back to face him. "Celebrate?"

"Mmm-hmm." Oh yes, he was enjoying that spark of temper and heat in her eyes immensely, as it happened to match his.

"You know that Irish accent you pretend not to have?" She put a hand on her hip. "It was there when you first called out, before you knew it was me. And you know what else? You didn't look in the mood to celebrate. You looked mad." She peered around him at the computer. "At that?"

"Nope." Setting down the plans and file, he reached down to sleep his screen, but hit Enter by mistake, sending the reply to the mystery e-mailer.

Furious at himself, he stared at the screen and uttered one concise oath.

"What?"

"Nothing." And it would be nothing, he'd see to it. Turning away from the computer, he forced a deep breath before leaning back against the wall to properly soak up the sight of Nicole. She wore hip-hugging black jeans and a plain black tank top that didn't quite meet the jeans. The peek-a-boo hints of bare, smooth skin decorated by a diamond twinkling from her belly button made his mouth water. She hadn't done much to her hair other than plow her fingers through it, and the only makeup she wore was a glittery lipgloss. She was attitude personified, and yet he suddenly, viciously, wanted to devour her. *Needed* to devour her. "What does it matter what mood I was in then? I'm in the mood to celebrate now."

"Well, I'm not."

Indeed. She seemed tempered and unguarded, and very undoctor-like. Something he'd have realized from the very first if lust hadn't slapped him in the face. He could see the strain in her eyes now, the unhappiness in the set of her mouth. "What's the matter with you?"

Lifting a shoulder, she looked away.

"Nicole?" Shocking how much he wanted to pull her close and cuddle. He, a man who'd never cuddled, or been cuddled, a day in his life. "Bad day at work?"

Another negligent shrug.

She was going to make him drag it out of her. Fine. He suddenly wanted to know badly enough to do so. "Did you...lose a patient?"

A sigh much too weighted for such a little thing escaped her. "Not today. Thankfully."

"Someone threaten to sue you?"

Her mouth curved. "Not today. Thankfully."

Hmm. A sense of humor under all that armor. He liked that. "Did you get an e-mail giving you a very unwelcome blast from your past?"

She studied him for a long moment, while he kicked himself for letting her slip past his guard enough that his mouth had run away with his good sense.

"Is that what happened to you?" she finally asked.

"We were talking about you."

"I don't want to talk about me." To prove it, she crossed her arms.

"Ah. You're a hoarder."

"A *what*?"

"You hoard your emotions. I appreciate that in a woman, as I do the same."

"That's not exactly something to be proud of."

"No kidding. If I had a dime for every time a woman tried to get me to open up and cry all over her..." His mouth curved. "Well, let's just say I'd be one wealthy man. So..." He cocked his head. "We're both in a mood, full of temper and restless energy. Might as well pool our resources, darlin'."

Her brows came together. The earrings up her ear glittered as she cocked her head. "Let me guess. We could pool resources in the way of, say...having wild animal sex, maybe up against that wall?"

God, she was something all riled up. Not to mention what image her words had just put in his head. "Well..."

"You're thinking about it, aren't you?"

"Oh, yeah, I am."

Cynicism hit her gaze now, and he had to be quick to reach out and grab her wrist when she would have whirled away. "I'm thinking about it, Nicole, because *you* said it. I'm a guy, we're visual creatures, and you just gave me one amazing visual."

"There it is again," she accused. "Your accent. It comes out with temper or..."

"Or...?"

"When you're..."

"When I'm what? Turned on?"

She crossed her arms over her chest. "You should know, I agreed to bring you the plans so I could tell you I'm not going to act on my attraction to you."

He felt heat spear him. "You're admitting to an attraction?"

The look on her face was priceless. "Oh, just forget it." She upped the ante by putting her hands on his chest. Staring down at her own fingers, she spread them wide, as if she wanted to touch as much of him as he could.

"What are you doing?" he asked a bit hoarsely.

"Pushing you away."

But she wasn't pushing.

Because he needed a grip and she wasn't providing one, he put his hands over hers, entwined their fingers.

She let out a slow breath, and he did the same. Then their gazes met.

"We should have just talked about our day," she said shakily.

"Mine sucked," he offered.

"Mine too."

"I got that blast from my past and I didn't like it."

"I got hit on by my boss."

"What blast—" she said, at the same time that he said, *"What?* What do you mean hit on by your boss?"

"Never mind—" They both started, then halted, stared at each other and let out a breath.

Then, inexplicably, Nicole's lips twitched.

His did too, and beneath his fingers, hers relaxed. Her smile, which came slow and surprisingly sweet, warmed him in a way he hadn't expected.

"How about we don't talk at all," she whispered, and leaned forward a very tiny fraction of an inch so that their mouths were lined up.

Lined up but not quite touching.

Ty ached to remedy that, but there was the matter of what had happened to her at work, something he found he couldn't let go. "Nicole, about your boss—"

"No talking," she said firmly.

"But—"

She put her fingers to his lips, which brought him back to the animal-sex thing.

With a little sigh, she leaned into his throat. "Damn it, you smell good. Who'd have thought you could smell good?"

She smelled good, too, so good he nearly took a bite out of her. "Why wouldn't you have thought so?"

"Because I really don't want to like you." Her eyes clouded. "You have no idea how much I don't want to like you."

"But you do."

She said nothing, and he smiled, pulling back far enough to look down at her. Sunlight sliced across half her face, illuminating her expressive eyes. "Listen up, darlin', because my accent is about to make a return."

With that he bent his head, slid his jaw to hers, then put his mouth at the sensitive spot beneath her ear. "I don't want to like you either. So damn much, I don't."

Having said that, he let out a slow breath to steady himself, and she shivered against him. "But it's too late. I already do." His fingers untangled from hers, so they could move up her back. "So let's use that to our advantage. Let's forget today." He plowed his fingers through her short, silky hair, holding her head in his palms.

Her eyes, hard and cynical only a few moments before, were wide as saucers as he tipped up her face. Lowering his, he repeated, "Forget today. Forget the stress."

She licked her lips. Swallowed hard.

And shot a hot ball of lust into his belly. "Hell," he said grimly. "Let's go for broke and forget our own names, what do you say?"

She sucked in her breath. "I never forget my name."

"That's because you're too logical." He was loving the way his touch seemed to interfere with her breathing. Through her tank top he could feel the outline of her nipples, tight and straining against the material of her shirt, dying for some attention. He was dying to give that attention. "Sometimes, Nicole, you just have to go with the flow."

"Going with the flow is not a strong suit of mine," she said a bit shakily.

"I'm beginning to see that."

She fisted her hand on his chest. "I don't like complications in my personal life, Ty."

"Complications can be a good thing. Temporary complications, of course." His voice lowered a fraction. "Are you ready?"

Looking a little wild, a little panicky, she chewed on her lower lip.

Stared at his mouth.

Arched her body just a little, just enough to drive him nearly right out of his living mind.

"Nicole? Are you ready?"

"Just do it."

"Do what?" he asked huskily, teasingly.

"Kiss me!"

She looked so frustrated he nearly laughed. Nearly. Because there was nothing funny about how turned on he was, about how much he wanted her. "As you wish."

Brushing his mouth over hers, he slid the tip of his tongue along the seam of her lips in tune to their twin moans.

And kept his promise as he made them both forget their names.

4

NICOLE'S HEART pounded in her chest as pleasure swept through her. She didn't know how she could be attracted to this man in this way, when he was the last person she figured she should want to feel such aching desire for.

They were polar opposites, for God's sake. She was tense, an overachiever, dedicated to her work over and beyond all else.

He was laid-back. Easygoing. Not exactly forthcoming with his real self.

Okay, so maybe they shared that last trait.

But what was it Taylor had said about him...he was willing to let life take him where it would. Here. There. Anywhere. Not her, she knew exactly where she wanted life to take her. She'd always known.

And where she wanted life to take her had nothing to do with a man. With sex. With *feeling*.

She wanted life to take her right along the same path she'd been going. She wanted to be a great doctor. She wanted to try new and innovative surgeries, and be successful at them. She wanted to save people's lives.

And not think about her own.

Yet there was no denying, he did something to her, something to her insides. He made her yearn and burn for human contact. Physical contact.

And that was something she rarely allowed herself because it made her open. Vulnerable.

She didn't like to be open and vulnerable.

But that's exactly what he did, without even laying a finger on her. He could have done it with just his eyes, but he had his hands on her now. She wanted to hate him for that, even as she wound her arms around his neck, even as she tilted her head for better access and kissed him back with everything she had.

Her body's immediate reaction surprised her. Consumed her. She certainly hadn't planned on feeling this aching desire, and for a man she hadn't yet decided to trust. Her fingers ran over the sexy tattoo on his arm, then up his slightly rough jaw. He ran his down her back. She slid her fingers into his short hair and gripped hard. He rocked their bodies together.

"This is insane," she decided.

"Yeah." With a sexy growl deep in his throat, he slipped his hands beneath the edging of her top so that his fingers played at the base of her spine, stroking over bare skin, while his mouth danced over hers again, making her do just what he'd said he could do. Making her forget today, forget the stress.

Forget her name.

She wanted to pull away, wanted never to have goaded him into this embrace. Hard to do, since she'd practically climbed up his half-nude body in a desperate attempt to get even closer.

End it, she told herself.

Instead, she continued to kiss him back with everything she had. Her tongue encouraged his, her hands claimed his sleek, muscled chest, while her insides melted at the hard, hot feel of him beneath her fingertips. She clung crazily to him as the only solid object in her frenzied world. And his lips...Lord, his lips! They were warm, firm and deliciously demanding. She could have said the same thing about his hands, which were at her waist now, his thumbs lightly caressing the quivering flesh just beneath her belly button. A knot deep inside her tightened. Her legs wobbled. And her nipples had long ago hardened to needy points, as if he'd already touched her there.

But he hadn't, and that she wanted him to more than she wanted her next breath no longer shocked her. She wanted this man.

Then, from somewhere behind them came the ping of a computer snapping her back to reality. For those glorious few moments he'd actually made her forget that she stood in his house, mewling all over him, practically begging him for something she was not prepared to give.

"Your computer is calling you," she said far more unevenly than she would have liked.

Still leaning over her, his mouth wet from hers, he slowly blinked, giving her a heavy-lidded look that made her want once again to melt all over him. "What?"

Pulling all the way free of his hands so she could get her brain functioning again, she stepped away, disturbed by how devastating one simple kiss had been.

Bottom line, when he laid on his easygoing charm, he was dangerous to her mental health, and this power seemed such an innate part of him she just needed to stay the hell away, period. "Your computer," she repeated, licking her lips and tasting him on her. "It's calling you."

It took him a while because first he watched her tongue dart out to lick her lips, but finally he turned his head and looked at his computer screen.

His breathing wasn't even either, Nicole noticed, just as she'd noticed every little detail about him. Like his bare chest, lightly tanned and hard with lean muscle. Or his faded, soft jeans, and the not-so-soft bulge behind the zipper.

She turned him on. The unexpected knowledge, along with the overwhelming and equally unexpected power of that, blew her away.

She turned him on. She, the original geek, turned

on the sexiest, most erotic, most sensuous, passionate man she'd ever met. And that shouldn't have been so...thrilling. "You have mail." Her voice sounded breathless again. Not good. If she wasn't careful, he'd notice and take it as an invitation. "Aren't you going to look?"

"Yeah." Blocking the screen with his big body, he read the e-mail, then put the computer on sleep mode. And though his face was carefully creased in one of his trademark easy, slow smiles, tension came off him in waves. "Where were we?" he asked in a light lilt that could have melted Iceland as he reached for her.

"Oh, no," she said, backing up, right into a wall. "Not so fast." She slapped a hand to his chest, his *bare* chest, which radiated heat. Her fingers started to curl into him, wanting more, so she wrenched it back. "I'm out of here."

"You going to let a little kiss bother you then?"

She lifted a finger and pointed it at him. "You are *not* going to goad me into another one."

"Because that would be...mind-blowing?"

"Because that would be...stupid." She ducked beneath his arms and moved to the center of his office. "I came here to give you the plans and tell you I'm not attracted to you."

"Which we've proved is a lie."

"Okay, so I don't *want* to be attracted to you," she amended. "And now I'm gone."

He waited until she got to the door. "Would it be so bad, Nicole, if we gave in to it?"

Not turning to him, not daring to, because at one look from him, she'd cave. Instead she tipped back her head and studied the ceiling. "Yes."

"Because...?"

"Because. Just because."

"We'd heat it up good, darlin', you know that."

Since her body was *still* heated up good, she had no doubt of that. Then his computer beeped again, accompanied by a surprisingly low and vicious oath from Ty. Turning back, she caught his unguarded expression as he reached for the keyboard.

Fury, plain and simple.

Wondering what was wrong, she sidled up behind him almost without realizing it, so that when he whipped around hiding the screen, she would have fallen backwards if he hadn't grabbed her around the waist.

Fingers gripping her tightly, he lifted a brow. "See anything interesting?"

"No."

His voice had lost all of its warmth. "You were right to run, Nicole. You *should* run. Now." He let go of her, and she stumbled back. By the time she regained her balance, he had turned away, hands fisted on the windowsill as he stared outside.

She stared at his stiff back. "I didn't see anything."

"You'll have to be quicker next time, huh?"

His temper stirred hers. Whirling, she stalked through the door, then down the hallway, and was reaching for the front door when he wrapped his long fingers around her elbow and spun her around. He had both his hands on her arms now, holding her still. He towered over her, her dark-haired, blue-eyed mystery man with the low, gruff voice and the sexy mouth that she was attracted to only every breathing moment she looked at him.

She struggled to free herself, but he wasn't having it. "I can bring you to your knees with one well-placed kick," she warned him.

"A moment ago I might have been in the mood for an all-out, drag-down, dirty fight, but not now." His hands gentled, and he used one to cup her face. "I snapped at you and I'm sorry."

"Fine."

He sighed at her unbending, rigid stance. "Look, I was feeling nasty, all right? And I tend to take it out on anyone around me." He sighed again. "Which is why I don't often have anyone around me."

She wanted to stay mad. Mad gave her energy to leave. But with him looking at her in that disarming way, with his hands still on her...it all dissolved.

"I'm sorry," he repeated softly.

"I said fine."

"Forgiven?"

She had to shake her head. "I'm usually so nasty when I'm not working, no one wants anything to do with me. My own family would rather I just— Damn it. *Damn it.*" She slapped her forehead. "I forgot to go to the family dinner my mom planned. There'll be hell to pay for that."

"Why?"

"You don't have a family like mine, I take it," she said wryly. "Big, bossy, noisy and more demanding than any work schedule I ever face."

"No, I don't have a family like that." His eyes were curiously flat again. "I don't have one at all."

No. No, that wouldn't tug at her either.

"I really am sorry," he said very quietly, cupping her face, letting his long fingers stroke her skin. "Don't let me and my foul mood chase you off."

"I...need to go."

"You know, I never would have pegged you for a chicken," he taunted softly, and stopped her in her tracks.

She put her finger to his chest. "Take that back." No one called her a chicken, and— And his chest...damn! His chest was captivating her all over again.

His smile reached his eyes again, when instead of

continuing to poke him she ended up dragging her finger in slow circles from one pec to the other. "I am not going to sleep with you," she said, but mmm, he had the best body. When her fingernail scraped over his nipple, he made a little hiss through his teeth. The sound shot straight to her good spots. "I'm not."

"There you go, your mind in the gutter again." His voice was a little rough around the edges now, even rougher when her finger ran over his nipple again.

"You weren't thinking it? Not even a little?" she whispered.

"Well, I know you were."

"I can lust after you and still keep my distance."

"Can you?"

"Watch me." She whirled to the door, put her hand on the handle, and...hesitated. "Are you...going to be okay?"

"Okay?"

"After that e-mail." She glanced at him, but he'd perfectly shuttered his expression.

"Don't you worry about me, darlin'."

She had the feeling no one did. He had no one, which was almost beyond her comprehension. Her own family was a regular pain in her ass. But they were also always there for her, no matter what, and always had been. She couldn't imagine being totally alone.

"I can see those wheels turn, doctor."

"I was just wondering how it was you came to be all alone. What happened to your family?"

"Personal questions? From you?" His smile seemed a little off. "Tell you what. I get a question for every one of yours. Let's start with this one. How is it you're so beautiful and sexy, and yet the fact that we turn each other on makes you nervous as hell?"

Beautiful? Sexy? Those weren't adjectives she attributed to herself. Brainy, yes. Technically minded, yes.

But sexy? The man needed glasses. Only there didn't seem to be a thing wrong with those amazing eyes of his. She opened the door to his soft laugh.

"Let me guess...you have work?"

"Right," she said. "Work."

All the way home it wasn't that mocking laugh of his that Nicole thought about, but the flash of a shocking emotion she'd never imagined from Ty Patrick O'Grady.

Vulnerability.

Ty WORKED the next few days as if he had a demon on his heels, and he did.

Her name was Dr. Nicole Mann.

But he was a man used to ignoring his emotions, and he could continue to do so through this job.

So why he made more trips to Taylor's building than was strictly required, he had no idea. Today was no exception. It was late afternoon, three days after The Kiss.

And damn, it had been some kiss. Truth was, he wanted another taste. He wanted her gripping him tightly, wanted her weak for him. He wanted her to care.

Odd, when *he* didn't want to care. God, how he needed not to care.

TAYLOR CAUGHT Nicole sneaking up the stairs to her loft apartment after a long day of work. "Hey, come in for a sec."

"Um...well..." As always, she thought longingly of her bed, and of her plans to be in it within ten minutes. Of the new medical reports in her arms that she was dying to dig into.

"Oh, save the puppy-dog eyes, I'm immune. You can't just work, read about work and sleep." Taylor crooked her finger, a gesture she expected to make people come running. "Come on and take your medicine like a woman, Dr. Mann. I've got Suzanne inside and she's so excited it's almost making me think there's something to this love crap after all."

"Then why don't *you* go get married?"

"Not in this lifetime. I told you, you and me, single forever. Now get in here. It's time to try on the dresses I got us for the engagement party."

Nicole wished she'd taken a double shift. "You didn't have to do that."

"Yes, I did. You'd have never gone to the store with me to try them on, and I know damn well you don't have a single dress worth a damn in your closet."

"Nicole, is that you?" Suzanne stuck her head out Taylor's door and grinned, her red hair piled on top of her head, her gorgeous lush body zipped into some shimmery black cocktail dress that made her look like a sex goddess. "What do you think?" She spread out her arms and turned in a slow circle. "Is Ryan going to like this?"

Having rarely seen Suzanne in anything other than her usual catering uniform of black bottoms and a white blouse, or her gauzy sundresses, Nicole shook her head in amazement. "Are you kidding? He's going to attack you on the spot. *I'm* attracted to you wearing that."

Suzanne laughed and pulled Nicole inside. "This is so much fun. Now for you..."

Rule number one, never let them take you inside.

"This is going to be good." Taylor rubbed her hands together and looked Nicole up and down. "Strip."

Nicole merely laughed at the command, but Taylor just crossed her arms and waited expectantly. Nicole's smile dissolved. "No. No way."

"Yes, way."

"Hey, stop that." Nicole held on to her shirt as Taylor tugged at it. "Get your paws off me."

"I got the perfect dress. Don't worry, it was on terrific sale at a discount outlet, since I know how cheap you are."

"How do you know that?"

"You live here, don't you? The dress is emerald green, sparkly and designed to drive men wild." She held up a shimmery piece of material that was far too small to possibly be a dress. "It'll show off your great body, though you're going to need a hell of a push-up bra."

"Gee, thanks." Nicole pulled off her shirt.

"You ought to think about buying a set of boobs," Taylor said, making Suzanne choke on her soda.

Nicole glared at Suzanne, who pressed her lips together and wisely refrained from so much as smiling.

"Hey," Taylor said, lifting her hands. "Just thinking out loud here."

"Why in the world would I want to do such a stupid thing as buy a set of breasts?" Nicole asked. "To catch a man? I don't want a man."

Taylor lifted a brow. "If you tell me you're interested in women—"

"I'm not a lesbian, you idiot." Nicole stepped out of her pants. "I'm just happy being alone, that's all."

"Yeah." For a moment Taylor looked inexplicably...sad. Because that was so unusual, Nicole almost asked her about it, but Taylor held out the green material. "Luckily, as I've always said, you don't have to be celibate to be single."

"Who said I was?" Nicole looked at the dress in her hands, and realized she had no idea how to get into it.

"So you're telling me you're getting some?" Taylor snatched back the dress, straightened it out and slipped it over Nicole's head. "You're too uptight and grumpy to be getting any. Unless you're giving him his and not getting yours."

Nicole pulled her face free. "*What?*"

Suzanne cleared her throat. "I think she means maybe you're giving him orgasms but he's not giving them to you in return."

Nicole divided a glance between the two woman, each watching her with such pity in their eyes, she had to laugh. "You're both nuts." She yanked the dress down her hips and quickly ran out of material.

"I see Ty looking at you," Taylor said casually, tapping a well-manicured nail on her perfectly painted lips.

Nicole pretended not to hear that.

"Ty?" Suzanne fussed with the straps of the dress at Nicole's shoulder. "Who's Ty?"

"My architect," Taylor said. "Remember? I told you about him. But since you were kissing Ryan at the time, you might have missed it." Taylor never took her eyes off Nicole. "He's tall, dark and sexy as hell. Not to mention his delicious, eat-me-alive accent."

"An accent can't be delicious," Nicole said, and both women laughed at her. "What? It can't."

"She's ga-ga over him," Taylor decided with delight.

"We'll have to invite him to the engagement party," Suzanne agreed.

"What?" Nicole got a bad, bad feeling as she smoothed down the dress. "Now why would you go and do that?" Both women were staring at her. "What now?" Self-conscious, she crossed her arms. "What are you staring at?"

"My God." Taylor shook her head. "I can't believe it."

"Wow." Suzanne sighed dreamily. "Just wow. You're beautiful, Nicole."

Nicole just stared at them, then laughed.

"You are," Taylor said softly.

Nicole shot them a last fulminating look, then stalked over to look into the antique stand-alone mirror Taylor had in one corner. What she saw made her jaw drop.

It wasn't often she slowed down enough even to look in a mirror. She dressed for comfort, wore little makeup and had her hair cut short for convenience. If she had to think about her looks, she saw herself in a white coat. Sexless, really.

She didn't look sexless now. The emerald color made her skin glow and brought out her eyes. Even her hair, usually worthless in the way of obeying or looking good, seemed...well, decent. Maybe more than decent. And her body...she actually had one.

"You have to wear it." Taylor said of the dress that clung to every inch of Nicole's form. The spaghetti straps held the snug bodice up in front, crisscrossed over her slim spine in back, where the dress dipped sinfully low. The hem came high on her thighs, and slipped higher with her every movement.

"You almost look like you've got boobs and hips," Taylor noted.

"You look gorgeous," Suzanne said, with a long look at Taylor. "You have such a beautiful body, Nicole."

"A little skinny." Taylor sniffed, but then smiled. "But some men go ape for a toned body like that."

Someone knocked at the front door, and while Taylor went to answer it, Suzanne said quietly, "You really do look amazing. This is going to be so much fun."

How to tell her she'd rather have a root canal? "I'm not wearing stockings or heels."

"Okay."

"I mean it. I—"

"You'll never guess who I found," Taylor said, coming back into the room. "A man. And just when we wanted a man's opinion, too. He just wanted to drop off some papers, but..." Smiling the smile of a cat with the canary's tail still hanging out of her mouth, Taylor moved aside.

Ty stood there, looking sweetly baffled. Until he saw Nicole, then all that sweet bafflement turned to heat as his eyes slowly took in the crazy dress she wore.

"What do you think?" Taylor asked Ty innocently. "Good enough for an engagement party?"

"Good enough to eat," Ty said, the Irish heavy in his voice.

5

THE LAST TIME Ty had seen Nicole she'd been walking away from him, and the taste of her had still been on his lips. He'd watched her go and decided not to do that to himself again.

No more watching.

Well, he was looking plenty now, wasn't he? Looking so hard he could see her every little breath, which seemed too quick and shallow for her to be half as calm as she was pretending, standing over there in that killer dress.

But hot as that bod was, it hadn't been the dress that nearly brought him to his knees. No, the look in her eyes had done that. The look that said "back off" and "want me," all in the same flash of those gray, gray eyes.

Suzanne and Taylor were grinning at him proudly, as if they'd personally created the vision standing before him.

"She does look good enough to eat, doesn't she?" Taylor said, clapping her hands. "Just wait until we get on the thigh-high stockings and do-me heels."

"Okay, I'm done." Nicole pointed a finger at Ty. "You. Stop staring. And you." She whirled on Taylor. "No stockings. No high heels that say do me or otherwise."

Ty did his best to stop staring as she turned her back on him to chew out Taylor, but as he caught a good sight of the rear view, he nearly swallowed his tongue. Now he could see why the stockings would have to be thigh high, the dress dipped so low he caught a peek-a-boo glimpse of her peach, silky-looking panties.

Nicole, rough-and-tumble ready, tomboy, warrior of her world...and she wore peach silky panties. If that didn't completely destroy him, he didn't know what did.

"I have got to get to work," she grumbled, bending for her discarded clothes and showing more peach silk.

Not that he was looking. Nope. Not looking—

She caught him looking. With a furious glance that singed the hair right off his arms, she stalked by, giving him a quick scent of shampoo and clean, very angry woman.

"Hey, I thought you decided to cut back your hours," Taylor called out to her. "So you don't kill yourself before you hit the big three-oh."

"No, *you* decided I should cut back my hours. I decided to stop trying to convince you I'm just fine."

"You're not fine." Taylor stood beside a nodding Suzanne for unity. "You live and breathe that job, without time for anything or anyone else. It's not right, Nicole. You're hiding out from life. Tell her, Ty."

Nicole dared him to say a word with stormy eyes.

He lifted his hands. "I don't—"

"Oh, please." Taylor pointed to Nicole's face. "See those dark circles under her eyes? Lack of sleep."

Ty hadn't slept well either, mostly from the memories of Nicole's mouth on his, from the feel of her body beneath his hands, from the little needy sounds that had escaped her throat before they'd broken apart for air.

Under the circumstances, with his own dark circles beneath his eyes, he didn't really feel he had the right to say anything.

"If I want a mother, I'll call mine," Nicole said.

"Which reminds me, yours came by." Taylor lifted a brow. "Checked me out. I must have passed muster, as she told me to make sure you get your sleep, eat your veggies and don't take extra shifts at the hospital."

Ty lifted his own brow at Nicole's impressive and colorful opinion of that. Then watched her very fine ass sashay to the door.

"Don't ruin that dress yanking it off," Taylor told her. "And use a hanger!"

The door slammed, and Taylor snickered.

Suzanne sighed. "You shouldn't have baited her that way."

"Are you kidding? If I didn't, she'd never have put the dress on, much less agreed to wear it. And she really does need to eat more veggies, you said so yourself."

"She didn't agree to wear the dress," Suzanne said.

"Oh, she'll wear it." Taylor tossed them both a positive smile. "She'll wear it with bells on."

Ty was just thankful he wouldn't have to see it. In fact, he was still thanking his lucky stars when Suzanne turned to him and said, "You'll be invited to the engagement party, of course."

"Me?" Panic was a taste he hadn't eaten in a good long time.

"Yeah. I think you're going to be around a while." Suzanne gave him a little smile.

Oh, boy. There were matchmaking plans in those eyes. Unintentionally, he backed up, making both women laugh.

"Don't tell me a man who wears clothes as well as you do has an aversion to dressing up like Nicole's?" Taylor said.

"No, but I do have an aversion to being set up."

"Set up?" Taylor cocked her head to the side. "Most men would be drooling to go out with a woman who looked the way Nicole just did."

"Not me. I get my own women, thank you. Didn't you want to show me your contractor bids? You wanted my opinion, right?" He could hear the desperation in his voice. "Can we get back to that?"

"We're not talking marriage here, Ty." When he didn't relax, Taylor just sighed. "Fine. I'll let you in on a little secret I think will help the situation here, all right? Nicole and I? We plan on remaining single. *Forever.* No white dress, no white cake and no diamonds on our ring fingers. If there's any hooking-up going on, it's of the one-night variety only. Follow?"

"But telling him that only gives him an unfair advantage over Nicole!" Suzanne protested.

Taylor kept her amused gaze on Ty. "I have a feeling he's the one who needs the handicap. Hurt her though," she said casually. "And we'll hurt you."

"Oh, definitely," Suzanne agreed.

They weren't serious, Ty thought. They couldn't be serious. He laughed to prove it.

They didn't laugh back.

"Actually," Taylor said seriously, "if you hurt her, we'll hunt you down and cut off your balls. So..." She clapped her hands and smiled. "Ready to get to work?"

American women were insane, he thought. Completely insane.

TWENTY MINUTES later, Nicole ran back out of her loft. She needed to lose herself in something, and the first thing to come to mind had been the hospital. Her mind was now firmly on work.

Okay, not true. Her mind was still wrapped around the way Ty had looked at her in that dress. Oh, man, how he'd looked at her in that dress. Her knees still were a little weak. Who'd have thought a man could have such heat in his eyes? She'd nearly imploded on the spot from the intensity.

But she was absolutely *not* going to waste time thinking about that, or analyzing her reaction to it. She was going to concentrate on work—

She came to an abrupt halt in front of her car. The streets were filled with shoppers and diners, with people who had nothing to do all day other than wander.

But Nicole had plenty to do. And she'd get to it, if sitting on the hood of her car hadn't been Taylor and...and the man she'd just promised herself she wouldn't think about.

Heads together, they were poring over an opened manila file and laughing. Until they saw her.

Well, Taylor kept laughing. But Ty's smile slowly faded. "You changed," he said.

"Yeah, it's hard to operate in a cocktail dress."

Taylor, who had her feet propped up on the bumper of Ty's car, which was parked right in front of Nicole's, waved her closer. "Ty is trying to help me decide on a contractor. These two right here?" She held up two different bids. "They're young and cute. And expensive. But very good at what they do, apparently." She looked at Ty for approval, who nodded. "And these two..." She switched papers around and held up two more bids. "They're a tad bit older, more experienced, slightly cheaper...but I guaran-ass-tee you, they'll have beer bellies and plumber cracks hanging out the backs of their low-riding jeans, and it won't be pretty."

Ty rolled his eyes. "Tell me you're not hiring a contractor based on his ass."

"Okay, I won't tell you." Grinning, she popped up, hugged Nicole, and started toward the building.

"Well, gee, I guess we're done," Ty said to her back, standing up himself.

Turning around, Taylor smiled. "I just figured, since Nicole didn't *really* have to be at work, and since I'd bet the bank she hasn't eaten, that the two of you could go out."

"No," Nicole said quickly. Too quickly, but damn it, she couldn't help it. Eat with Ty? No. No way.

But Taylor danced her bossy butt into the building and vanished.

Ty reached for Nicole's hand, tugging her close enough that he could look into her face. "Hey," he said softly.

"Hey."

"Sorry about upstairs."

"You mean about staring at me in that dress?"

His mouth quirked. "Not for staring, no. Sorry you were so uncomfortable in it. You looked...amazing."

"Yeah. Funny what a low-cut, tight number like that does for a man. Did you lose a lot of brain cells?"

He let out one of those slow, dangerous smiles. Dangerous, because she couldn't take her eyes off it. That, combined with his warm hand in hers, and suddenly she stood there on the sidewalk, completely forgetting she didn't want to stand there with him. Staring at him.

"Darlin'," he said, "I lose brain cells every time I look at you."

His voice melted her all the more. Unfair, very unfair. "Well, if this does it for you..." She gestured down to her military-green cargo pants and plain white T-shirt. "Then you have even bigger problems than I thought."

His see-all blue eyes never left hers. "It has nothing to do with what you're wearing. Or how you look."

Oh, God. Why did he say such things? No one had ever said such things to her, and she had no idea how to handle it. If she'd been hands deep in an emergency surgery, or up to her eyeballs in X rays...*those* she could handle.

But this wasn't work, this was far more personal

than work had ever been, and she was at an utter loss. She inhaled a breath and held it.

"Yeah," he said. "Scary shit, huh? Let's go eat, Nicole."

"Because Taylor said to?"

"Because I can't get you out of my head. We might as well spend some time together and see where it goes."

"It's going nowhere."

He smiled again. "Let's go see."

"No." She fumbled for her car door, slid in. "I've really got to go." She turned the key.

And the engine simply coughed.

She turned it again, with more force, but she got that ridiculous wheezing noise that told her the battery was dead. Again. "Damn it."

"Sounds like battery trouble." Easy as he pleased, he opened her door, tugged her out. "Lucky for you, my car runs like a sweetie. I'll drop you off at the hospital, then charge your battery while you're at work."

"I don't want—"

"It's no trouble."

Naturally he didn't take her right to work, but stopped at a cute little sidewalk café a few blocks away. "For sustenance," he explained as he got out and came around for her.

Came around for her. Nicole stared at him as he led

them to a table, while she tried to remember the last guy who'd opened a door for her.

Or put his hand lightly on the base of her spine, touching her as they walked.

Her skin still tickled. That it wasn't an entirely unpleasant experience had her head spinning. "Who are you?" she said over the table, bewildered, which wasn't a common problem for her.

He lowered his menu and smiled. "What you see is what you get."

"Why do I sincerely doubt that?"

"I don't know. What about you? Is what you see what you get?"

She glanced down at her plain clothes, ran a finger over the silver hoops in her ear and lifted a shoulder. "I think so."

"Tell me about the earrings. What do they mean?"

"How do you know they mean something?"

"A hunch," he said, which she didn't like, because it was true.

How did he seem to know her so well? "There's one small hoop for every year of medical school," she admitted. Her own personal badges of honor, during a difficult time when she'd been struggling to survive in a fast-paced, adult world while still in her late teens.

With a slow smile that bound her to him in a way she didn't understand any more than the ease with which he seemed to know her, he lifted the sleeve on his own shirt, revealing the tattoo she'd seen before. It was a narrow band around his tanned, sinewy bicep in a design that was incredibly sexy. Just like the rest of him.

"I got a part of it for every year I made it through college," he said. "Finished it when I graduated and started my internship in Sydney."

"Badge of honor," she whispered, and at this unexpected common ground of a deep, soul-felt connection, she felt herself warm to him in a new, different way.

The waitress came, and when Nicole tried to order just coffee, Ty took over and ordered enough food for an entire third-world country.

"I'm a growing boy," he said with a shrug and a big, unrepentant grin. "And besides, I promised Taylor I'd feed you."

"Is that why we're here? Because you promised Taylor?"

His smiled faded, but before he could speak, the waitress came back with bread and butter. When she was gone, he grabbed a piece of bread and said, "We're here because I wanted to spend time with you." He slathered butter on the hot bread. "And I think, behind all that cool-as-ice stubborn orneriness, you want to spend time with me as well." He handed her the bread.

"This is *not* headed to the bedroom." She took his offering because the butter was melting all over, making her stomach growl. "Not yours *or* mine."

"Of course not." He sank his teeth into his own piece of bread. "You have to go to work."

She took in his innocent gaze. "I mean ever. This isn't going to the bedroom, yours or mine, *ever*."

"Well, now, that's just a crying shame, given how combustive we are just sitting here, much less kissing."

Hearing him say it, in the Irish accent he didn't acknowledge, made her pulse quicken. "We need to forget that kiss."

Now he laughed, the sound rich and easy.

"We do," she protested.

"Much as I'd like to oblige you, darlin', I'm going to be around. A lot. We're going to run into each other. Nobody's going to be forgetting anything."

"You've thought about this."

"Hell yeah, I've thought about this." His eyes were crystal-clear, and very intent on hers. "Last night I decided never to so much as look at you again."

"What happened?"

"What happened?" He shook his head, and as the waitress come back with their order he dug in with a gusto that forced her to do the same. "*You* happened."

Since she didn't intend to touch that statement with

a ten-foot pole, they ate in silence. Nicole had to admit, it felt good to fill her belly. How she managed to forget to eat so often was beyond her, but she liked this feeling of...satisfaction. Since she intended to deny herself any other kind of satisfaction—say sex with Ty, with which she was quite certain he would have no trouble satisfying her—food would have to do.

"So." After inhaling enough food for an army—where did he put it all in that long, hard body?—he leaned back in his chair. "What's up for today, doc?"

"Surgeries. Meetings. More surgeries."

"Are you good?"

"The best."

He smiled. "I bet you are. Did you always know this is what you wanted?"

"From day one." She wondered the same about him. "Were you always going to be an architect?"

Some of his good humor faded, just a little. So little, in fact, she thought maybe she'd imagined it. "Not always," he said lightly.

When she just looked at him, he sighed. "Let's just say I didn't have the most auspicious of beginnings."

She felt a smile tugging at her lips. "A troublemaker, were you?"

"Of the highest ranking."

"I'm shocked. Were you—"

"Oh, no. This is about you." He lifted a brow. "Your mom is something."

Nicole stared at him. "You met her, too?"

"Darlin', the way she stormed the building, everyone met her. What a dynamo." He smiled. "You're like her."

"I am not."

His smile went to a full-fledged grin. "Are too."

She set down her fork. "She has a bazillion kids, a husband, two bazillion grandchildren and runs her world like Attila the Hun."

"Yeah, you share that last part. So what was it like, growing up with such a large family?"

He wasn't just idly asking, he'd leaned forward, his entire attention on her face. He really wanted to know. "Well..." She thought about it. "I never had my own bed. And I had to wait hours for the bathroom. Oh, and I wore a lot of hand-me-downs." She hesitated, then admitted, "But there was always someone around when I needed them." Always. And, she also had to admit, she hadn't thanked any of them enough for it. "What about you?"

He suddenly didn't look so open. "I already told you, I don't have a family."

"What happened?" she asked quietly.

"Well, I never knew my father, and let's just say my mother is better off forgotten." Expression closed, he reached for his iced tea. "Need a refill?"

"No, thank you." Behind his nonchalance, she saw his regret, and a sadness she couldn't reach. But more than that, pain. "Ty—"

"Don't," he said softly. "Please, don't."

Before she could respond, he tossed some money on the table and stood. "Let's get you to work."

"And after that?"

His light-blue eyes gave nothing of himself away now. "What do you want to happen after that?"

"If I said nothing?"

"I'm not sure I'd believe it."

"Ty—"

"Look, Nicole...do we have to figure it out right now?" He touched her cheek, let out a smile that was short of his usual levity. "Do we really have to decide right this very minute?"

With a shake of her head, she took his offered hand, and shocking herself, tipped her face up when he leaned in for a sweet kiss. Or what *should* have been a sweet kiss, but was instead only an appetizer.

He pulled back, and she opened her eyes. There was a question in his, but she shook her head. "Work," she said.

"Work, then." And he took her outside.

Work would be good. At work she could bury her thoughts and concentrate on what mattered. Her job.

Not the man who had unexpected depths and a touch she couldn't seem to forget.

AND SHE DID MANAGE to bury herself in work. The emergency department was overloaded due to a strange and violent outbreak of a flu, which had severely dehydrated an older woman to the point that her kidneys failed. After that, they'd taken out an appendix from a hockey player, and then sewn a finger back on a carpenter who'd managed to cut it off with his table saw.

By the end of the shift she'd nearly managed to forget all about Ty. As she stood in front of a vending machine in the reception area of the hospital on her way out the door, her cell phone rang.

"Honey, I dropped off some food for you. Your nice landlady let me in, so I stuck it in your fridge."

"Mom." Nicole had to laugh. "I have food."

"No, you had a rotting head of lettuce and two sodas. Now you have food. Taylor is very beautiful, isn't she? Is she married? I didn't see a ring, but—"

"*Mom*—"

"Just say thank you, Nicole."

"Thank you, Nicole."

"Funny. Don't forget to come to dinner this Sunday."

"I'll try."

"Try harder than last Sunday. I'll even shamelessly bribe you. I'll make you brownies. Your favorite."

"Mom—"

"*Double* fudge brownies."

Nicole had to laugh. No matter how long and bloody her day had been, her mother never failed to bully a smile out of her. With her mom, she always felt warm and loved, even when she wasn't warm and lovable at all.

And some people never had this in their life. Some people, like Ty. "I love you, Mom."

"Well." Her mother's voice got thick, and she sniffed. "I love you, too, baby. See you soon."

"See you soon," she promised, then sighed. She would have to make sure she did before her mother showed up at her place with more food she wouldn't eat.

Her eye on the chocolate caramel bar in the vending machine, she put a dollar in.

It ate the money and didn't spit out the candy.

"Why you—" She kicked it. This had always worked in the past, but now the machine mocked her with silence.

"You have to have the right touch." Dr. Lincoln Watts glided his body directly up behind hers, so close that she nearly choked on his expensive aftershave. His arms surrounded her as he reached past her to punch in the buttons on the machine.

The candy bar dropped.

Nicole stepped forward until she was practically kissing the machine before she turned in his arms.

"Thank you." He had until the count of three before she used her fists.

"Now you owe me." There was a little smile on his lips that she was certain he considered sexy, but it creeped her out. No wonder all the nurses hated him.

She'd already changed back into her own clothes, and his eyes were eating her up. "Do you have any interesting tattoos to go with all those earrings of yours?" he asked a little huskily.

She stared at him. "Is that an official question?"

"Go out with me tonight."

"Dr. Watts—"

"Linc," he corrected gently, with a not-so-gentle look in his eye as he stroked her cheek.

She pushed his hand away, met his gaze to make sure he saw her anger, and spoke carefully so as to not confuse the idiot. "I don't go out with people from work. I don't mix work and my personal life. Ever."

"I'm not 'people.' I'm a doctor."

"I don't care if you clean bedpans, my answer is the same."

His jaw tightened. His eyes became distinctly not so friendly. "You're turning me down again?"

What was it with too-smart, too-good-looking men? "Yes. I'm turning you down. Again."

"That's a bad plan, Nicole."

"Dr. Mann."

He looked her over for a long moment, then stepped back, his eyes ice. "I can make your life hell here. You know that."

"No, I can make *your* life hell." God, she hoped that was true.

She was the youngest doctor on board, the newest, and she wasn't naive enough to forget there were hidden politics in force, or that Dr. Lincoln Watts had all the strings to pull and she had none.

Still, she kept her head up high as she walked past him and out the doors of the hospital. That she had just now remembered she didn't have her car made a perfectly bad ending to a perfectly bad day. Spoiling for a fight, with no one to go nose-to-nose with, she stalked over to a pay phone to look for the number of a cab company.

6

DRAWING AND DESIGNING were what Ty had been born to do. Envision and create, and then move on.

He was good at it, especially the moving on part. He could do it right now, just pack up and go. Hell, he didn't have anything he couldn't buy again. In fact, he had moving down to a science. He could pack up and get out of anywhere within a half hour if he had to.

But Taylor's building, while appearing to be a dump, had huge potential, and the job stirred his creative juices enough that he didn't feel like thinking about moving on, not yet.

At the moment he stood on the roof, staring down at the third-floor living-room window—Nicole's window to be exact—trying to figure out a way to pop it out a little to fit the early-1900s traditional facade of the place. The challenge excited him, and he retrieved his notepad from his pocket and hunkered down, yanking the cap off his pen with his teeth so that he could write. He was a page into it when he heard the screech of tires.

Nicole slammed out of a cab, which reminded him he'd fixed her car for her. He took one look at the strut in her walk, at the fury pouring off her in waves, and wondered what had happened to make her look as though she was spoiling for a fight.

Though he still had measurements to take in the rafters, he told himself he could come back later, and shimmied down from the roof to the mock balcony in front of her living-room window. He'd just landed on his feet when he saw her clearly through the glass, stalking in her front door. Slamming it. She saw him immediately, he could tell by the slight narrowing of her eyes—ah, how lovely to be so welcomed.

With a kick-ass attitude he couldn't miss, she headed toward him, opening the window so fast he thought for a moment she meant to push him down three stories to his death.

"What are you doing here?" she demanded.

"Just thought I'd drop in."

"Funny," she said without a smile. "You hang outside windows often?"

"Just yours." He cocked his head at the unmistakable unhappiness in her gaze. "You going to invite me in?"

"Nope."

"What if I say please real nice?"

"Oh, fine." She turned away. "Suit yourself, you're going to anyway."

Yes, he was. And her stress drew him like a magnet. He threw a leg over the sill, climbed through and straightened, studying her stiff spine. Coming up behind her, he put his hands on her shoulders.

"Shh," he said when she flinched, and gently began to knead at the knots she had in her neck. There was a virtual rock quarry there, not to mention the heat of the rage she was so carefully controlling. Given how much of the world she took on her shoulders on a daily basis, her stress level had to be off the charts. He ached for her.

But in spite of his genuine need to soothe and comfort, there was more. Beneath her white shirt he could see a hint of yellow lace bra, and he wondered if her panties matched. "How did you get so tense today, doc?"

"I tend to get that way when some asshole puts his hands on me uninvited."

He went still.

"Not you," she said.

Still, Ty suddenly felt very tense himself. "Who put his hands on you uninvited?"

She lifted a slim shoulder. "Just some jerk at work."

"Your boss again?"

Another lift of her shoulder.

"Goddammit." Now he was trying to control *his* temper, but he had to do it. She didn't want his anger, and she sure as hell didn't want compassion, so what was he supposed to do with all this unexpected violence? Keeping his voice light took about all he had. "Do I need to go caveman for you and kick some serious butt?"

That startled a laugh out of her, a genuine one, and he relaxed slightly, keeping his hands working on her neck. If she'd been hurt, she wouldn't be laughing.

"I handled it," she assured him.

"Yeah, well, I hope you kicked his balls into next week."

"Nah, just his ego."

She said this very proudly, and that made him smile. "Good girl." He dug for more taut muscles, thinking she was so petite beneath his fingers, so...perfect. "Sure I can't go reinforce it?"

"No way." She was quiet a moment, biting her lip as he started on a kink at the base of her shoulder blade.

He didn't want her to bite her lip, he wanted her to let out the helpless moan, wanted her to give him a sign that he was making her feel good, that he was helping her let go of all the fury, but apparently he couldn't have everything he wanted.

"Ty?" she said softly after a moment.

"Hmm?"

"Thanks." Turning to face him, her lips curved.

"You know, for having caveman tendencies and wanting to go bash in a head and all."

The way she was looking at him made him want to beat his chest with his fists and howl at the moon. He'd meant to stay away from her. Why the hell hadn't he stayed away? "Nicole?"

While most of her anger had faded, she still had a good amount of wariness in those jaded eyes. "Yeah?"

"I'm going to put my hands on you."

"You already have."

"More hands."

"Why are you announcing this?"

"So you don't kick *my* balls or ego into next week, warrior princess." Cupping her face, he tilted it up. Slowly. Giving her plenty of time to settle in.

Or back away.

She didn't back away, but neither did she settle in. Instead, she stiffened, just a little, just enough to break his heart. "No, don't get all tight again." His lips whispered against hers. "I'm going to kiss you now. Say yes."

"Ty—"

"Yes or no, Nicole. I don't want you to mistake me for any other asshole doing this without permission."

"I—I know who you are."

"Yes or no."

"Yes. Okay? Yes! Put your hands on me." Her arms

snaked up around his neck. Fisted in his hair. "Kiss it all away, Ty. Can you do that?"

"Oh yeah." His hands slid from her face to her hips and he pulled her close. "I can do that."

She went up on her tiptoes to meet him halfway as he covered her mouth with his, cutting off anything else hanging between them, of which there was plenty. With a rough, appreciative groan, he invaded her mouth with one sure glide of his tongue, figuring she'd either kiss him back or belt him one.

She kissed him back. In fact, she mewled and arched her body to his like a cat in heat. His arms banded around her more tightly, lifting her off the ground as his mouth slashed across hers in a fiery kiss that only left him needing more, more, more. And when they finally broke apart, she staggered back, placed a hand over her heart and licked her wet lips. "What the hell was that?"

"Not sure." He hauled her back against him. "Let's try it again and see if we can figure it out."

"Hmm." Then they were kissing again, tongues caressing and plundering, hands touching anywhere they could land as they ate each other up.

Ty had never felt anything as fast and as hot and as combustive as this. Her hands pushed up his shirt. He shoved up her light shirt. She kicked off her shoes, went up on her tiptoes and hooked a leg around his hip, straining against the biggest erection he'd ever sported.

Never letting go of her mouth, he had his hands up her shirt and she had hers on his zipper when the *beep, beep, beep* of her pager nearly jerked his heart right out of his chest. "Don't listen," he said against her lips, gripping her at the waist to hold her still.

With a soft little moan, she opened her eyes. "I have to."

"Nicole—"

"I have to." Stepping back, she licked her lips again, as if she needed that very last taste of him, and pulled down her shirt with fingers that trembled. She avoided his gaze as she went looking for the offending beeper. "I'm sorry. I shouldn't have let it go that far."

"There were two of us inhaling each other."

"Still, I should have—" She looked down at the pager.

"Let me guess. You have to go."

"Yeah."

"Yeah." He backed away, shoving his hands in his pockets to keep them off her. "Goodbye, Nicole."

"I'm sorry."

"Me, too." And he left before she could count off each and every reason why they should never have let anything like this happen.

He already knew every single one of them.

He just couldn't remember why they mattered.

SOMETIME IN THE MIDDLE of the night Ty gave up staring at the ceiling and went into his office. Not one to waste precious hours, he sat at his desk and decided he'd work off the restlessness.

Okay, horniness.

He should have kept his hands and mouth to himself. Should have, would have, could have.

Regrets? Is that what he felt, when he'd promised himself to never have them? Never to look back? *Live life to its fullest*, he'd always told himself. *Get everything you want, and smile all the way to the bank as you do it.*

It turned out it was no easier to work with a hard-on than it had been to sleep with one. So he turned on his computer, where he found another e-mail from his friendly stranger.

Dear Ty Patrick O'Grady of Dublin,

You asked who I am. Of course you want to know! I'm Margaret Mary Mulligan of Dublin. I'm twenty-four years of age, and I'm also the daughter of Anne Mary Mulligan.

Which makes me your half sister.

Actually, I'm not sure about the half part because I don't know who my father is. Our mother, as you probably know, is dead.

You're my only family. I want to know you. Please write back.

Margaret Mary

Ty stared at the e-mail for so long the words leaped and jumped in front of him. A sister? He had a sister?

Was it even possible?

He thought of his mother, professional trouble-seeker, professional man-screwer, and knew it was entirely possible. With a sigh, he hit Reply.

Dear Margaret Mary...

Ty sat there, fingers poised over the keys, and couldn't figure out what he wanted to say. *How are you?* Too formal.

How about *What do you want from me?* Nah, too defensive.

Dear Margaret Mary. Of Dublin.

He stopped to laugh. So formal, this mystery half sister. But then his smile faded. This could only bring trouble and rotten memories, neither of which he wanted. Thinking that, he typed:

Why now? Why me?

Besides, there could be a dozen of us for all I know.

Maybe you should try one of them.

Ty Patrick O'Grady

He hit Send, then sat there staring at nothing for who knew how long, until his computer beeped, indicating an incoming e-mail.

"So you can't sleep either," he murmured and leaned forward.

Dear Ty,

I'm so glad you wrote. You have questions, questions are good.

But there is no one else. She told me herself before she died. Not that her word ever meant anything, but on this, I want to believe her.

It's just you and me.

Aren't you even curious?

Margaret Mary

Curious? Hell, no. He'd rather not think about his past at all. He'd rather look around him and see where he was right this moment. How far he'd come. And he'd come pretty damn far.

It's just you and me.

Damn her for that, for putting it into words so simply. So strongly. Clearly she didn't relish being alone, as he did.

She was young, very young, and probably had idealistic hopes about a family around her, hopes he'd never entertained for himself.

Ah, hell. He hit Reply.

> Margaret Mary,
> If you're looking for family to be a comfort, forget it. I didn't get the comfort gene. If you're looking for a handout, you'd have better luck with our mum herself, dead or otherwise.
> Best leave it alone.
>   Ty Patrick O'Grady

He hit Send. It was the right thing to do, he'd been on his own so long he didn't have any business opening his life to another person.

He *was* a loner, through and through. No family, no long-term lover. And if he gave a fleeting thought to what it might be like to be different, to let Margaret Mary in, to let Nicole in, he let it go.

Not his thing. Besides, he didn't know how to let anyone in.

Since he couldn't seem to sleep or entertain himself, he figured he might as well start his day. That meant pulling out the plans he was working up for Taylor's building.

It was the attic that was concerning him today, as Taylor had fond hopes of a place to store all the antiques she couldn't seem to stop collecting. The last time he'd been there, he'd gotten distracted by Nicole.

Seeing as Nicole was no doubt killing herself at work, he decided the crack of dawn was a perfectly fine time to crawl around in the attic to his heart's content without disturbing a soul.

And he did just that, getting filthy in the process as he crawled through spiderwebs the size of his car. Straddling a beam, he pulled out his pad, and was happily making notes when he heard a door open. The sound came so close, he looked around, baffled, until he realized it was the apartment door directly beneath him.

Nicole's.

Because of the way the building was built—on a slight incline—the roof was really on two different tiers. On the higher level was the attic. Right next to that, but a full level below, was the loft apartment. There were two ways into the attic, the way he'd come in, through the third-floor hallway, or through a trap door at the far corner of Nicole's living room.

Due to a vicious storm only a few months ago, when a tree had fallen through the bedroom area of the loft, much of that part of the roof had been re-done. But not the attic portion, which was still incredibly rickety. Reaching down, he opened the trap door.

It made a loud creaking sound, but Nicole, standing just inside her front door, never looked up. Ty realized this was because she had on a set of head-phones, which, given the volume of her singing—so off-key he had to smile—meant she couldn't hear anything.

Before he could attract her attention, she'd kicked off her shoes, then crossed her arms in front of her and whipped off her top.

She wore a tiger-striped bra—did she have any idea how sexy her secret lingerie fetish was?—and then put her hands to the button on her pants. Oh, boy. "Nicole!" He was barely braced on the studs now, but he leaned over way farther than he should, knowing he had to make her see him or she'd be good and pissed by the time she was naked, and generally he liked his women soft and smiling and mewling with lust when they were naked.

Still singing, she shucked her pants, kicking them across the room with an abandon that normally would have made him grin.

Her panties did not match her bra. They were pur-ple, lacy and very, very tiny. Turning in circles in a lit-tle shimmy of a dance, she headed toward her bed-room, giving him a good, long look at her backside as she wriggled and shook.

"Oh man," he whispered to himself, and leaned out as far as he dared. "Nicole—"

He crashed right through the ceiling. The air

whipped his face; the floor rushed up to greet him, but all he saw was a tiger-striped bra and purple lace panties.

NOT MUCH SCARED Nicole. But Ty falling through her ceiling shook her to the core. By the time she reached him, which took longer than it should have since she wasted five seconds just staring at the huge mass of him on her floor, he hadn't budged.

"Oh my God, Ty. *Ty.*"

He was on his side, face gray through all the drywall dust. Dropping to her knees at his hip, she leaned over him. "Ty, can you hear me?"

Nothing. But she could see his chest rising and falling, and she nearly sobbed in relief. "Okay. You're going to be okay. You are."

Surging up, she grabbed her portable phone, dialed for an ambulance; calm, cool, in control. As she always was in an emergency.

Then she looked down at the big, handsome, far-too-still man on her floor and wanted to fall apart. Her hands shook as she gently put them on him. What to do? God, what to do? Every ounce of medical training she'd ever had flew right out the window. "Damn it, get it together, Nicole." She ran her hands down his limbs, frowning at his right ankle. Not broken, she didn't think, but already swollen. Then she got to his right side, and the possibly cracked ribs, and had to take a deep, calming breath. "You're going to be okay," she whispered, having no idea which of them she was talking to.

There was a huge knot forming on his head, and he hadn't regained consciousness. "Ty." She cupped his face, his beautiful, too-still face, with the long dark lashes and strong, sharp jaw. "Come on, Ty. Come back to me. Wake up." She checked his pupils. Uneven. Concussion, if he was lucky. "Please, Ty. Please wake up. For me, do it for me, okay? Wake up and I'll—"

He groaned. Coughed. Rolled from his side to his back and groaned again, eyes still closed. "Shh, darlin'," he said in a rough whisper. "It's too early to be yelling."

"Ty." Her eyes burned with the relief. "You're back."

"You...didn't finish your sentence. What will...you do...if I wake up?"

That he could joke, even now, horrified her. Then he tried to sit up, his face in a grimace of agony as he held his head.

"Don't move," she said in a rush, helping him lie back. He'd turned green. "You might have broken something, at the very least your big fat head. *Don't*," she repeated when he kept trying. "Just hang on a damn second."

"Shh," he begged, eyes still closed. "No noise."

"Are you nauseous?"

He cracked one eye open, ran it over her, then closed it again. "I am, yes. Though I refuse to puke on the very lovely underwear you're wearing. You're so pretty, Nicole." He sighed, then went utterly still and silent, terrifying her.

"Ty!"

"Yeah, here." He didn't open his eyes. "Did you know that when you say my name in that soft, sexy voice of yours, I almost wish we were going to go for it. You and me."

"Ty—" But a sudden pounding at her front door had her leaping up, reaching for her clothes. "Hold on!" she called, hopping back into her pants.

"Nicole?" Taylor knocked louder. "Honey, what was that crash?"

Nicole pulled on her shirt and hauled open the door. "Ty fell through my ceiling. The ambulance is coming. Oh, God, Taylor, look at him. He hit his head, he's concussed, and I can't remember what to do!"

Taylor grabbed her hand and ran toward Ty. "Oh, you poor, big, sexy baby. You're not going to be sick all over my floor, are you?"

Ty choked out a laugh that ended on a groan and some fairly inventive bad words.

"Don't make him talk," Nicole begged, ridiculously panicked. It was just a bump on the noggin. Lord knew, his head was hard enough to handle it.

Taylor grabbed Nicole's shoulders and gave her a little shake. "I'll go wait for the ambulance. Stay with him." She hugged her hard. "It'll be okay, honey."

"That's my line," Nicole whispered as Taylor ran out, leaving her with the big, bad, broken Ty lying at her feet.

7

NICOLE WENT IN the ambulance with Ty. Took him into ER herself and spewed out orders.

Hovered and tried not to wring her hands. Tried to focus on what she was doing. They took care of his bruised ribs, his sprained ankle. Noted his concussion, which worried her the most.

Yes, his head was big and hard. But damn, he'd hit it hard.

She dealt with the staff and their curious expressions, knowing she'd shown her hand when she'd yelled out directions in a wobbly voice.

She'd never yelled while on duty.

Well, the staff would get over it. The question was, would she?

She filled out Ty's paperwork, which was more time-consuming than she'd ever realized, being on the other side of the fence for the first time.

Taylor was in the waiting room, looking unusually scattered and stressed. Suzanne was there too, leaning on the tall, dark, gorgeous Ryan, who had his arms around her in a way that made Nicole take a moment. Had she ever leaned on a man like that? Ever had a man who wanted her to? Ever been offered true affection from a man?

Nope. But then again, she'd never wanted such things. She didn't want them now. Not when she was strong enough to stand on her own two feet.

When she could convince them to go, she sent Taylor, Suzanne and Ryan home, promising them Ty—and his hard head—was in good hands and going to be fine.

And he would be. She would see to it, all by herself.

TWO HOURS LATER, Nicole sank to the cot at Ty's hip and stared at the sleeping, still far too pale man.

With the proper care and rest, he was going to be fine.

But when was *she* going to be fine?

He'd gotten under her skin. There was no other excuse for her ridiculous panic at the apartment. None.

Outside the cubicle, machines bleeped, footsteps squeaked, voices carried, some raised, some hushed. There were smells too: antiseptics, medicine and the scent of fear and pain. Normal ER sounds and smells.

But inside the cubicle, life seemed suspended. It was just the two of them, one unconscious, the other wondering what had happened to her life. Lightly, she reached out and touched the bandage on Ty's head. "You scared the hell out of me, Ty Patrick O'Grady," she whispered.

"Of Dublin," he said in a heavy Irish brogue without opening his eyes.

Had he really spoken, or was she hallucinating on top of everything else? "Ty?"

"You scare me, too." His voice sounded raspy, and more than a little goofy from the drugs they'd given him for the pain. "You and my sister both. I have a sister, did I tell you?"

"No." She covered her mouth to keep her hysterical, relieved laugh in. "You haven't told me much about yourself at all."

"She found me on the Internet. Wants to know me. Everyone wants to know me." His words were slurred, but the Irish lilt was unmistakable. So was his sudden crooked grin, though he still didn't open his eyes. "You want me, too, don't you, doc? You want me as much as I want you. Say it for me."

Her heart leapt in a new sort of panic. "Keep your mouth zipped, you big idiot, you're drugged."

"Is that why my body is floating away from my head? Your head is floating, too, doc. You're so pretty. Makes me wish I could stay in one place for once, you know that?"

"Please...please, shut up or you're going to say something you'll regret." She wanted to run, and she wanted him to keep talking.

"You do want me. I know you do."

How the rough-and-tough man could lie there looking so adorable in his cockiness was beyond her. "Ty."

He let out a long sigh. "Maybe that's just me with all the wanting then." He sighed again. "You're screwing with my head, all three of you."

Three? He was worse off than she'd thought. That, or he'd had too many drugs. Leaning in close, she checked his pupils, making him grin. "I'm okay, darlin'. Sweet of you to worry though."

She sat back. "This sister...you talked to her?"

"She wants a family, but who the hell needs family? I don't need anyone. I haven't since I was fifteen and on my own."

She went very still on the outside while her heart did a slow roll. "That still only makes two, Ty. Your sister and me."

"But then there's *her*."

"Her who?" If he said he had a wife she'd have to kill him.

"My mother. She didn't want me. I probably never told you that."

Nicole sighed and put her hand on his chest. Her own ached like hell. "No."

"I'm a bad seed. Probably should have warned you before now, but I didn't want to scare you off. The truth is, you name it, and I did it. Stole clothes, stole food— Am I upsetting you?" he asked, opening his eyes to see hers welling up.

"Ty. *Rest*," she begged, wanting to wrap herself around him.

"Can't. There's someone jackhammering in my head. I didn't even know I had a sister."

"I know," she said in response to his baffled voice, stroking him with her hands, trying to quiet him because she didn't want to hear this, didn't want to know about him because, damn it, how was she supposed to keep her distance if she knew about him? "Please, Ty, I want you to—"

"I don't want to like her." After that statement, he was quiet for so long she thought he'd fallen asleep, and she just sat there, soaking him up. She'd imagined he'd had a rough childhood, but she hadn't imagined it as bad as it must have been. Because she couldn't help herself, she touched him, ran a hand over his arm, his jaw, wishing she could take his pain as her own.

"You feeling sorry for me, doc? Cuz if you are, I'm going to tackle you down right here, right now, and kiss us both stupid."

"You're in no position for tackling, much less kissing."

"Try me," he warned, and reached for her, missing by a mile. "Damn."

"Ty." She touched his pale, pale face. "Lie still."

"Yeah." Sweat broke out on his forehead. "Lying still now."

"Good, because you've got to save your energy for healing. You need to—"

"Nicole? Darlin'?" He closed his eyes tight. "I'd love to hear the lecture, really. But if you don't mind, I'm going to puke now."

THE NEXT TIME Ty opened his eyes, he was still in a damn hospital bed. Still in a far-too-small hospital gown with no back. Still feeling green and shaky and in too much damn pain to believe that the shot some mean nurse had given him a short time ago had worked.

He hated hospitals with an unreasonable vengeance, and had ever since he'd been twelve and was beaten within an inch of life. His own fault. He'd broken into a restaurant, only to get caught by the owner as he'd been stuffing his face with food from the fridge. Didn't matter that he'd been starving, or was a skinny little runt, the guy had gone berserk. The beating had landed Ty in the emergency room, where he'd been treated like little more than the wild animal he was. Once there, he'd barely outwitted the juvenile authorities. All he remembered, when he let himself think about it, was a vicious, snarling, vivid, Technicolor pain and the bitter stench of his own fear.

Now, being in another hospital brought it all back, quite unpleasantly.

Nicole's face floated into view above his own: her wide, expressive gray eyes, the short-cropped hair that so suited her arresting face, and the silver hoops up one ear. Then there was that mouth, with the full lips he so enjoyed nibbling on.

Another hallucination? He'd had some doozies since he'd been here, all of them involving her tiger-striped bra and purple panties.

"Hey," she said, sounding very doctor-like. She wore a white coat and had a stethoscope looped around her neck. How official. "How are you feeling?" she asked. "Still nauseous?"

In all the other hallucinations, she hadn't talked, she'd just smiled all sultry-like and had bent over his body, giving him pleasure such as he'd never known. "I like the other outfit better," he said, closing his eyes.

"What?" She put her hand on his forehead.

She thought he was still out of it. "Never mind. Let's blow this Popsicle stand."

"No can do."

He stopped in the act of tossing his blankets aside. "Doc?"

She clutched a clipboard to her chest, looking very in control in her own environment. Bully for her, but he wanted control in *his* own environment, thank you very much, and lying flat on his back in a scanty gown wasn't doing it for him.

"You need to stay overnight for observation, Ty."

"I don't think so." He sent her a tight smile. "Hand me my clothes."

"I mean it."

"So do I. Hand me my clothes or get an eyeful, and believe me, the gown hides nothing." Carefully, trying not to let out the pathetic moan he wanted to, he got himself in a sitting position. His ribs were on fire, so was his ankle, and his head...well, the pain in his head didn't bear thinking about because if he did, he was going to toss his cookies again. Since the good doctor, sexy as hell in all her disapproval, was glaring at him instead of handing him his things, he put his feet to the floor.

"Ty, don't be stupid."

"More stupid than falling through your ceiling, you mean?"

"You're still drugged. You can't get yourself dressed much less get yourself home."

"I don't feel drugged."

"Really? How many fingers am I holding up?"

He squinted at her hand. She had no fingers. And now that he took a good look, her head was separated from her body. A shame, really, because it was such a beautiful head. Bossy and stubborn, but beautiful.

"Ty? How many?"

"I'm not sure. But I can tell you you're wearing a tiger-striped bra and purple silky panties."

She didn't look amused.

Ty returned to his efforts of getting up. He looked at his ankle. Just touching it to the floor hurt enough that he had to suck in a breath. "Sure this thing isn't broken?"

"Just badly bruised."

Okay, then. Moving on. Next move—getting upright. With that feat in mind, he leaned his weight forward.

Dr. Sexy crossed her arms and frowned.

With a grunt of effort, he went for it, and surged to his feet. Or foot, as he held his screaming ankle off the ground. Ribs burning, head feeling like it had blown right off, he thrust out his arms for balance. The back of his gown flapped cool air on his bare ass.

As he waved wildly, Nicole tossed down her clipboard and leapt toward him. "Damn it." She shoved her shoulder beneath his arm, taking his weight, which, given how little she was, had to be considerable. "What the hell is wrong with you, you stubborn—"

"Shh." He wrapped his arm around her, gasping for breath as everything in his vision faded to a spotted gray. For a cold, clammy, sweaty moment he thought he was going to pass out, but the litany coming from the woman supporting him kept him conscious.

"Of all the idiotic, moronic…"

The ringing in his ears drowned out the rest of her monologue as she sat him back down, but he got the gist. He also got the pain. Holy shit, he hadn't imagined he could feel anything so much, but every muscle in his body had started a mutiny. Unable to hold back a low groan, he rolled to his side and panted for air.

"I'm going to call the nurse and get you another painkiller."

"Don't. She's mean."

"Baby."

He laughed, then nearly cried at the fire in his ribs.

"I wouldn't laugh," she advised, but there was something in her voice now, something… He managed to crane his neck and peer over his shoulder. Yep, that was his ass hanging right out for the world to see. He closed his eyes. "You getting a good view?"

She tossed his blanket over him. "I'm a doctor. I've seen it all."

"Yeah, well, this isn't quite how I imagined you seeing me. Nicole, I'm not staying here overnight."

"But—"

"I'm not," he said, and looked up at her. "I…can't."

"Why not?"

"I hate hospitals."

"Everyone says that."

"But I mean it."

She stared at him for a long moment, then sighed and sat next to him. "Okay, so you have a hospital phobia—"

"I'm not staying."

"You can't go home alone, you'll need someone to watch over you, help you."

Much as that went against the grain, he had to agree with her, if only for the simple fact that he couldn't even see straight. "For how long?"

"At least tonight and all day tomorrow. Maybe even a second night. After your hard head improves, then you can hobble around on your own if you're careful."

"Fine."

"Who's going to help you?"

"I'll figure it out."

She crossed her arms. "I know you don't have any family you'll call."

That cleared some of the haze from his vision. "Really? How do you know that?"

"You...told me."

Given the look of compassion in her gaze, he'd told her plenty. Terrific. "You listened to the ramblings of a drugged man?"

"You were happy enough to let your mouth run."

What had he said? "Did I mention anything about your interesting lingerie fetish? Because I have to tell you, Nicole, I find it fascinating that you're so tough and impenetrable on the outside, and so..." A smile curved his lips. "So incredibly soft on the inside."

"You're changing the subject."

"I'm trying."

She blew out a breath. "You didn't say anything embarrassing, if that's what you're worried about. You just said...you had a sister you didn't know about and that she was e-mailing you."

"And...?"

"Just that...your mother didn't want you."

Hell. He'd spilled his guts all over her. Her voice had softened, and that was definitely pity on her face. He didn't want her pity, he didn't want anyone's pity. He wanted out of this bed and he wanted that now. "Well. This has been fun."

She held him down with a hand to his shoulder. "I'm sorry, Ty."

For what? he wondered. Falling through her ceiling or for being so pathetic as to have his own mother cast him aside? "This isn't your problem."

She nodded, agreeing, and turned away. Made it to the door, which she studied for a long minute, as if fascinated by the wood. Then she turned around. "I know you're alone. That you're too proud to ask any friends for help. As a doctor, I can't release you knowing that."

"I'm leaving, Nicole, come hell or high water."

"I know." She closed her eyes. Opened them again and leveled them right on him. "Which is why you're coming home with me."

SHE WAS CRAZY. Or so Nicole told herself the entire drive home with Ty dozing next to her. She let Suzanne and Taylor fuss over getting him up the stairs. She gave him another pain pill, which he bitched about like a two-year-old but finally took when she threatened to pull out a needle instead.

Then she settled him in her bed and stepped back, wondering why just his pale face made her want to fuss. She'd never fussed a day in her life.

Ty looked around at the no-frills bedroom with the bare walls, at the bed with its navy-blue comforter and two pillows, and not a thing out of place except on the chair in the corner, which held some clothes and a perilous stack of medical journals. "Not even a romance novel to read?"

"I have those." She gestured to the journals and he shook his head.

"I guess I'm not surprised," he said. "God forbid you actually take time off when you're off. So. You're really giving up the bed for me?"

"You didn't like the hospital, remember?"

"Hmm."

Nicole glared at him. "What does that mean? What's wrong with the bed?"

He blinked sexy eyes at her. Waggled his eyebrows suggestively. "You're not in it."

Wasn't he something. "I'm taking the couch, big guy."

"You don't have a couch, you have an ancient, scary-looking futon masquerading as a couch. The only other thing you have out there is a nice-size hole in your ceiling and a mess on your floor."

"Nothing that can't be fixed." She did have the futon, ancient or otherwise, and put together with a blanket, she'd be fine. "Goodnight, Ty."

He leaned back against her pillows and looked at the ceiling, his faced lined with pain. "Aren't you going to read me a bedtime story?"

"Sure. Once upon a time there was this idiot who fell through a ceiling and landed on his head."

He closed his eyes. "Ha ha."

"So why are you afraid of hospitals?"

"I just don't like them, all right?"

"All right." He didn't look at her, didn't move a muscle, and yet she *knew* in that moment his pain was more in memory than physical. "Look, don't get too comfy. I'll be waking you every few hours."

He cracked open an eye. "Is that a promise?"

"To check on your hard head, Ace."

"I got something else you could check on."

"Uh-huh, and with all the drugs in you, it'd work really well, too."

A ghost of a cocky smile played around his mouth. "Try me."

"Goodnight, Ty."

"'Night. Nicole?"

At the door already, she turned.

"Why did you take me home with you?"

She lifted a shoulder. "Because you were hurt."

"*Truth.*"

She sighed. "I don't know why."

He nodded, and closed his eyes again. Almost immediately, his breathing evened out as the drugs finally claimed him.

For a long moment Nicole stood there, just staring at him. She had a man in her bed, when she'd never put one there before, much less *yearned* for one. There'd always been too much to do, too many people to save.

Now he lay in her bed, and she was yearning. Yearning and hurting at the same time, because he'd never get serious. Oh, she believed he was serious about getting into her purple panties.

But for him, this was simple lust.

That scared her. It scared her because she thought maybe, just maybe, she could feel more than that in return.

NICOLE DIDN'T GO to sleep, but kept herself busy, mostly continuing to watch her patient. She swept up some of the mess in her living room. She cleaned out whatever was growing in her fridge, and she reassured Taylor and Suzanne that Ty was fine. Twice. After an hour and a half, she sat at his hip, munching on a bag of pretzels. "Ty?"

He didn't budge.

"Ty?"

"I knew you'd be back, begging me to take you."

"I'm here to check on you."

"Then check on me." His voice was groggy but there was nothing groggy in those eyes when they opened and watched her with an intensity that made her squirm.

"How are you feeling?"

"I'd feel better if you stopped sucking on that pretzel. It's making my blood drain southward."

"You're fine," she decided, swallowing the pretzel and leaving him to go back to sleep, which he did instantly.

She went to the living room and proceeded to watch the clock tick. After another hour, she went into the bedroom again. Moonlight streamed over the bed, highlighting the long, lean form lying there. He'd kicked off the covers. He was sprawled on his back, one arm over his eyes; his big chest rose and fell evenly. She knew this because he wore only a pair of boxer briefs, ribbed cotton, charcoal-gray.

They fit him snugly just below his navel. He was bruised and cut over a good portion of his torso. He also had scars that had nothing to do with his fall. A long, nasty-looking one low on his flat belly that looked like a knife wound. A puckered one near his collarbone that looked like an old burn, and another on his arm. There was a long scar down one muscled calf, and another on his thigh. And then there was the tattoo he'd shown her—an intricate design winding around his left bicep.

And he called *her* a warrior.

She had bits and pieces of him now, and had put together a picture of how he'd grown up and become the man he was. There were still quite a few pieces of the puzzle missing, but he wouldn't welcome her curiosity. She shouldn't feel that curiosity at all, but did. He'd raised himself, a fact she couldn't deny made him all the more fascinating.

How could his mother, any mother, turn her back on a child? What kind of mother did that, let her own son think she didn't want him?

That it hurt her, hurt her for him, was another concern. She shouldn't feel this way, this possessive, protective way. He certainly wouldn't want it, nor, for that matter, would he want her compassion. He was far too proud for that.

And yet she couldn't tear her eyes off his beautiful

form. So she sank to the bed at his side and wondered what the hell she was going to do with him.

"You going to watch me sleep all night?"

She jumped back up, pressed nervous hands to her stomach. "You're awake."

"Want to see how awake?"

Since he was talking with his eyes closed, very carefully not moving a muscle, she smiled. "Do you know where you are?"

"In your bed. Without you." His voice was low, husky. Unbearably sexy. "Want to check anything else? My temperature maybe? I'm hot, darlin'. Really hot."

"You're hurt."

"Not that hurt."

She eyed him. He still hadn't moved a single muscle. And suddenly, the doctor inside her vanished, replaced by a mischievous woman who knew she was safe. "You don't think so? You really think you could...?"

"I know it."

"Yeah? Then prove it. Come get me, big guy."

He pried a bleary eye open, closed it again when she sent him a cocky smile.

"Come on, come get it," she dared, making him groan.

"Can't you help a man out a little and come down here?"

"Nope."

"Ah, now see, that's just plain old mean."

"Goodnight, Ty."

"We already said that."

"We're going to say it several more times yet tonight. You can thank your concussion for that."

He swore colorfully, making her smile again. A man who could put together those descriptive words was going to be okay.

The next time she checked on him, he was in such obvious discomfort and pain she ended up sleeping in a chair at his side to watch over him more closely. In the deep of the night, he shifted, then groaned, and she was there, reaching out to touch, to soothe. Though he didn't say a word, she knew he was awake, and terribly uncomfortable. "I'm sorry," she whispered.

"Me, too. I'm sorry I fell through your ceiling. I'm *really* sorry I did that."

"Need another pain pill?"

"Yeah. I've decided I like those."

"And the doctor? How about her?" She had no idea why she asked, and held her breath, wishing she could take it back.

But a weak smile touched his mouth. "Maybe I decided I like the doctor more than a little."

"That's only because I'm holding the goods."

His eyes opened at that. "You have the goods all right."

She blushed. *Blushed.*

"And I'm not talking about your tight little hot bod either, Dr. Nicole Mann."

She had no answer for that, but as he drifted off, none seemed to be required.

BY MORNING Nicole was the hoarse, groggy one. Since when had one single patient taken so much out of her?

Since she cared. Too much.

But she had an even more pressing problem at the moment. She wasn't convinced Ty could handle the day by himself. He hadn't yet managed to get out of the bed without her support, and though he did keep up a healthy stream of come-ons, she knew damn well he was all talk and no go.

So she did it. For the first time in her entire professional life, she picked up the phone and took the day off.

And wondered if she'd gone completely off the deep end.

8

AFTER SHE'D CALLED in to the hospital, Nicole stood in the middle of her living room, idle. *Idle.*

What was she going to do with herself with only one patient to take care of?

The entire day loomed large in front of her, when she'd never allowed herself a leisurely moment in her life. With a shrug, she pulled up a stack of medical journals and other related work reports she could read.

But for the first time since she could remember, they didn't appeal. So she sat in front of the TV she'd turned on only a few times since she'd purchased it several years ago.

And in no time flat, discovered the utter, addictive joy of daytime television. With the remote in hand, she clicked back and forth between *Bewitched, I Love Lucy* and *Court TV.*

Then the phone rang, annoying her. So did her caller.

"Hello." The lazily cultured voice was Dr. Lincoln Watts. "Slacking off today?"

Nicole's finger tightened on the phone. "I'm entitled to call in."

"Did you stay up too late?" His voice lowered. "Or did your lover keep you in bed this morning?"

"I won't be in today, Dr. Watts. That's all that concerns you. *Period*," she said with shocking calm, and because the commercial was over and *I Love Lucy* was starting again, she hung up the phone. She stared at her hand on the remote and realized she was shaking with fury.

Not even two seconds later came the knock on her door. Damn it. She got up, and gaze still locked on the TV, opened the door.

"Morning." Suzanne held a covered tray that smelled so delicious Nicole promptly forgot about the TV.

"Not for you." Suzanne slapped Nicole's hand when she went to lift the cover. "For Ty. Tell him I hope he's feeling better."

"You brought Ty food and not me?"

"Yes, and don't cheat him by eating any of it. He needs his strength to heal." She whistled slowly at the hole in the ceiling of the living room. "That poor, poor baby."

"He's not a baby." Nope, as Nicole had now seen just about every inch of his long, hard, perfectly formed body, she could say that for certain. "And food doesn't heal." She lifted her chin. "My skills as a doctor are going to do that."

Suzanne shot her a look of pity. "Oh, honey, have you got a lot to learn about men. There's only one way to reach them, and it's not, contrary to popular belief, through their penises. It's through their stomachs. Now give him this tray with a nice morning smile and you'll see what I mean. You *can* smile this early, can't you?"

Nicole glared at her.

Suzanne laughed. "Well, honestly, I don't see you smile that often. Actually, I don't see you do anything but work."

"Not today. I called in."

"You...*called in?*" Suzanne slapped a hand to her mouth in disbelief. *"You?"*

Nicole rolled her eyes. "It's not that big a deal."

"To you it is. You, the workaholic, took a day off to care for Ty. That's huge."

"He *did* fall through my ceiling."

"You took a day off." Suzanne marveled at that for a moment. "Wait until Taylor hears you're falling for him. She's going to be the last one of us holding on to that vow of singlehood."

"Oh no." Nicole laughed. Fall for Ty? *Ha!* "I don't know what you think is going on here, but you can just wash it right out of your hair. I'm staying single forever, just like Taylor."

"Uh-huh."

"I am." She meant it. Ty would finish his job here and sooner or later he'd be gone. Long gone. He wouldn't so much as look back, as looking back wasn't in his genes.

She wouldn't look back either, she'd—

She'd miss him. Damn it. She'd really miss him.

But she'd carved out a good life for herself. She had her career, a family that was only slightly dysfunctional, and friends, even if they were nosy as hell. She had all she needed.

"I used to be in denial, too," Suzanne said with a knowing smile.

"It's not denial."

"Right. Hey, I'll come back later for the tray and any details you want to share."

"There won't be details."

But Suzanne had already walked away. "Damn it," Nicole muttered when Suzanne's laughter floated back up the stairs. Shrugging it off, she went back to her shows.

And wondered if Ty was dreaming of her.

TY CAME AWAKE in slow degrees. When he was fully conscious, he carefully opened his eyes.

The sun rudely pierced into the room, stabbing him with the brightness until he closed his eyes again. He took mental stock and decided his entire body felt as if he'd been thrown under a steamroller.

Except for his head. His head felt as if he'd put it into a giant vise and cinched it down.

With no little amount of struggle, he managed to get to a sitting position. From there he eyed the bathroom door, only a few feet away.

It might as well have been a hundred miles. Determined, he staggered up, and for his efforts, nearly passed out. Gripping the back of a chair, he took a handful of deep, careful breaths. Daggers shot upward from his ankle. His ribs screamed. He had no doubt his head was going to fall right off. But he made it to the bathroom, shut the door and leaned back against it.

"Ty!" From the other side of the door came Nicole's worried voice. "What are you doing!"

"Considering getting sick."

"Are you okay? Are you hurting? Do you need any help?"

"No, yes and no."

"Ty—"

When he was done, he opened the door, about two seconds away from passing out.

Nicole was right there, wrapping herself around him, taking his weight. "Of all the fool things to do, getting up by yourself, trying to walk, moving around as if you didn't drop yourself on your head just yesterday..."

"Not back to bed," he said when she turned him that way. "Not unless you're coming, too."

Her arms were around his bare middle, carefully avoiding his hurt ribs. He liked the feel of her hands on him. Too much. She took him to the living room where he could see the blanket strewn over the futon. An episode of *I Dream Of Jeanie* was on TV. Next to the futon was a half-eaten bowl of cereal.

"Are those Frosted Flakes?" His mouth started to water. "And I love that show."

"It's a Jeanie marathon. This is the one where she gets stuck in her bottle." She looked at the TV. "I think I'd like to be able to toss my ponytail and have my every wish come true. You've just missed *I Love Lucy*. She was working on a candy assembly line. Honest to God, I've never laughed so hard...what?" she asked self-consciously as he stared at her.

It was just that her eyes were laughing. Her cheeks were flushed. And her hands were still on him. Irresistible combo. He found his insides stirring, and not just the part of him that usually stirred while staring at a beautiful woman, but something in his chest. She looked...*happy.* It wasn't a look he'd seen on her before, making him realize he hadn't often seen her outside of work mode.

He liked this side of her, he liked it a lot. "You haven't seen these shows a hundred times?"

"Are you kidding?" She laughed, a sweet, simple sound. "We weren't allowed to watch anything but public television growing up. I never even had a TV until a couple of years ago, but I rarely turn it on. I can't believe what I've been missing. And *The Brady Bunch!* What a crack-up—" She narrowed her eyes when he grinned. "Stop that."

"You're pretty damn adorable, Dr. Dweeb."

Her mouth opened, then shut. "I never know how to take you," she finally said.

"Take me any way you want, darlin', just take me."

She stepped back, which left him holding up his own body. He braced his legs, shooting an arrow of pain from his ankle directly to his ribs. Clutching them made his vision waver again and he gritted his teeth.

"You fool," she said softly, reaching for him again, easing him down. "Sit. Lucky for you Suzanne took pity and brought you a tray of food."

"You mean you aren't going to slave over a hot stove for me?"

"I don't slave over a hot stove for anyone."

"Hence the Frosted Flakes."

"Hence the Frosted Flakes," she agreed. "Pouring milk into a bowl, now *that* I can do." Shrugging, she set a heavenly smelling tray on his lap. "I think I missed the girlie gene. I don't cook, I don't sew, and..." She lifted a napkin Suzanne had folded into a flower. "I sure as hell don't fold napkins into shapes."

It took an effort to smile when his head was pounding, but she looked so unexpectedly vulnerable, he tried. "I like you anyway."

She didn't smile back, but she didn't slug him either. "You do?"

"Yeah, I do." She hadn't turned out to be anything as he'd imagined. She wasn't aloof or spoiled, or insensitive, but was warm and giving and incredibly compassionate. In fact, he had to resist the urge to pull her close and bury his face in her hair. Not only would it hurt like hell to do so, but the urge was wrong. He had no business feeling this way, none at all. "I think you're a pretty incredible woman, Nicole. And sexy as hell to boot."

She let out a deprecatory smile. "I've never been accused of being sexy before."

"Then you're not listening, because I've been thinking you're the sexiest woman I know from the first time I set eyes on you."

"Well." Brushing her hands on her jeans, she backed away, looking around her as if searching for someway to keep her hands busy. "I've got to..."

When she just turned in a slow circle, at a complete loss, he wanted to laugh. "Work?" he finished for her.

"No. No work today. I, uh..." She avoided his gaze, lifted the lids off the food Suzanne had left him. "Here. You need food before you get more pain meds."

Obediently he picked up a fork, groaning at an ache in his shoulder. Definitely he was getting too old to be falling through ceilings. "Why no work today?" He saw the truth in her eyes and gaped at her. "You called in? For me?"

"Well, what were you going to do? Make your own breakfast?"

"You didn't make breakfast," he pointed out, moaning again, this time at the taste of Suzanne's home-fried potatoes melting in his mouth.

"You complaining?"

"Nope, not at all." He took another bite, studied her. "You took a day off for me. I think you're crazy about me."

"Shut up and eat."

"Yeah. Okay." He shoveled in more food. "Thanks," he said into her inscrutable gaze. "For taking care of me."

"Yeah, well, don't get excited. I would have done the same for a stray puppy."

Oh, yeah. She was crazy about him.

NICOLE HAD never known the guilty pleasure of a day off. She'd heard her co-workers talk about how they occasionally stayed home simply to brain-rest, doing nothing more than eating junk food and watching soap operas all day long, and she'd always felt a sort of superior smugness about not feeling the need to do the same.

Soap operas. *Please.*

But—and she couldn't quite believe it—they were wonderful. She sat on the floor, cross-legged, in a ratty old pair of sweats and a comfy tank top, cradling a bowl of popcorn in one hand and the remote in the other. On the futon above her, crashed out cold, slept Ty.

It was odd, the feeling of contentment. Odd and terrifying.

When someone—two nosy someones—knocked at her door, she rolled her eyes. "You know, this is getting insulting," she whispered as she opened the door and faced Suzanne and Taylor. "I can take care of him."

Suzanne passed her a tray, probably loaded with lunch, because heaven forbid "poor baby Ty" starve to death with Nicole's inability to so much as toast bread. "Frosted Flakes three times a day is not nutritious."

Taylor grinned. "And...don't take this wrong...but we're not quite sure you know how to take care of a *man.*"

"He's not a man, he's my patient."

"I think he'd say differently." Taylor held out a laptop computer to her. "Tell him I locked up his car, but this was in it and I thought maybe he'd want it."

"He's not going to work, I won't let him." Nicole knelt to put the tray of food on the floor beside the door before rising to take the computer.

"Really." Taylor lifted that superior blond brow and gave her a knowing, far-too-self-righteous smile. "Know what I think?"

"If I say yes, will you go away?" Nicole asked.

"I think Suzanne's right," Taylor said. "I think I'm in danger of being the last one holding out for permanent singlehood."

Suzanne nodded while Nicole sputtered. She kept her voice low with great effort. "Just because I don't think he should work doesn't mean—"

"Honey." Suzanne put her hand on Nicole's arm and sent her a sweet smile. "It's okay you're after him."

"I'm *not* after him," Nicole said through her teeth. She jabbed a finger toward Taylor. "And I'm still firmly single."

"Okay, but just remember, you can stay single and still have wild monkey sex—"

Nicole slapped a hand over Taylor's mouth, glancing over her shoulder to make sure Ty was still asleep. "Okay, you guys have to go now."

"Why?" Taylor tried to peer past Nicole. "You get him naked yet?"

"Goodbye." Nicole tried to push them out of the way of the door so she could close it.

But Taylor kept her nose in the way. "Just one peek—"

"Goodbye," Nicole said firmly and put her hand on Taylor's face to hold her out as she finally closed the door.

Her relief was short-lived.

Ty had turned his head toward her. His eyes were open. Clear.

Curious.

"Hey." She came forward, wondering how much he'd overheard. "How's the head? You doing okay?"

"You could have told them you had me *nearly* naked but don't know what to do with me."

He'd heard it all. Perfect. "Oh, I know what to do with you," she assured him. "I just..." She stopped the teasing words because his eyes had gone so hot it caused a mirroring flame inside her.

For just a moment she wondered what it would be like to let him kiss her again, this time allowing him to peel off her clothes and make love to her. Eager for exactly that, her body actually leaned toward him in a show of willingness, but she had to remember, he was destined to walk away.

At least she was smart enough to know that wouldn't work for her, walking away. "I just..."

"Come here, Nicole."

He was sprawled on the futon. A light blanket covered his long legs and lap, but had fallen away from the rest of him, leaving his chest and arms bare. Bare and roped with muscles.

And bruises. "Are you feeling better, Ty?"

"Are you coming here?"

She pressed back against the door. "No, that's not such a good idea right now."

His eyes were still hot but he just lifted a shoulder, the fact he was too weary to move working in her favor. "I'll take the laptop."

She held it to her chest. "I don't think you should work."

"I don't think you should worry about it."

If she'd fallen on her head she'd probably be feeling nasty, too, so she gave in. Sort of. "Come get it," she said, holding it out.

"Come and get it?" he repeated incredulously.

"That's right."

"You're into S and M, right?" He struggled to his feet, and the blanket fell away from him. His shorts were low on his hips, and for some reason, her gaze attached itself to that area of his body and couldn't be torn away.

Then she caught him trying to hide his grimace of

pain, and she had to lock her hands on the computer in order not to rush over there and do something stupid, like touch him.

"When I get over there," he warned her grimly, trying to straighten. "I'm going to—"

"Fine." Damn him, he looked so pale. "Here." She moved toward him before he took a single step and gently pushed him back down, putting the computer on his lap. "Work. I don't care."

"Fine."

"Fine." She turned away. "I'll just..." What? Suzanne had just provided lunch. What else was there to do?

You could stare at him all day.

"I don't suppose you'd do me a favor," he said a little gruffly.

She turned back. "I am *not* helping you take a shower."

He stared at her for a flash before letting out a laugh that ended in a quick grab to his ribs and a groan. "Measurements," he grounded out. "I need you to go downstairs and measure a few things for me so I can get something done while I'm wasting your day." He hadn't bothered to cover himself back up. The sight of a nearly nude male body shouldn't have stirred her, not when she saw such things all the time.

But she had to admit, it wasn't every patient that had a body like his.

"Can you do that?" he asked.

"I suppose." He shouldn't work, but who the hell was she to mother the stubborn man? They didn't have a relationship or a commitment. He'd never get serious enough to have a commitment. And it wasn't as if they cared about each other.

Okay, *she* cared. Knowing that, and because she needed to get away from the sight of him for a few minutes, she snatched the paper he offered her out of his hands and headed toward the door.

"You'll need a measuring tape," he called out. "And be careful when you—"

"I think I can manage a few measurements." Taylor would have a measuring tape. And Suzanne would have ice cream. Because damn if she didn't need something good and fattening to take her mind off the other craving she had.

For one Ty Patrick O'Grady.

BECAUSE NICOLE was hoping Ty had gone back to sleep, and because she had to make sure she was entirely under control before she saw him again, she took her time about getting the measurements he needed.

And if she stopped at Suzanne's apartment and

mooched three brownies and a scoop of ice cream off her first, who was going to care?

Except her jeans.

When she finally walked back into her apartment, the living room was empty. So was the kitchen.

She found him on her bed. His laptop was open and hooked up to her phone line. He had his e-mail program open but his eyes were not.

"Ty?"

He didn't budge. He was sprawled on his back, his head turned slightly away, his chest rose and fell evenly with his deep breathing. Bruises bloomed on one side, and because he once again hadn't bothered with covers, she could quite clearly see his swollen ankle. He needed to ice that, and probably take more meds, she thought, moving closer. She'd just check his vitals first, and—

And the e-mail caught her eye.

Dear Ty,

I'm not looking for comfort or a hand-out. And leaving it alone was never an option.

We're family, linked by blood. Can you really say you're not interested? You have such a full life that you don't need this, the only other living relative you have?

I have a lot to offer, and I want to meet you. I want to know you. I want to be family.

I'm staying at the local youth hostel if you are interested.

Please, *please* be interested.

                                        Margaret Mary.

Nicole stared at the letter, her heart in her throat at Margaret Mary's raw need. And if *she'd* felt it, what had Ty felt?

"Did you see enough?"

Nicole nearly leapt out of her skin. Looking groggy, sleepy, unrested and irritable, Ty struggled to get up.

"No," she said, reaching for him. "Just stay—"

He slapped the computer closed. "Yeah, I'll stay. I'll stay the hell out of your way. If you'll stay out of mine."

9

NICOLE STARED at Ty as he got to his feet and very carefully straightened.

"Where did that come from?" she asked.

"Forget it." He looked around. "Where are my clothes?"

"Right there," she said, pointing to the folded stack on her nightstand. "But—"

"I have stuff I have to take care of." He grabbed his pants, then looked at them with a pained expression, as if he knew getting them on was going to hurt like hell. Jaw tight, he shook them out, then bent slightly at the waist. Sweat broke out on his brow and he wavered for a second.

"Oh, Ty. Get back in bed."

"Since I doubt that's an invitation," he said, his voice more than a little strained, "I'll pass, thanks."

"I don't get it. Your options were staying in the hospital for observation or coming home with me. You agreed, so what's changed?"

"I told you. I have things to do."

"Like go to the youth hostel?"

His head whipped toward her.

"I, um..." She clasped her hands together and rocked back on her heels. "I saw more of the e-mail than I meant to."

"You see more of everything than you're meant to."

"What does that mean?"

"Nothing." He waved away her efforts to help him, though he had to sit back down to work his pants up. By the time he stood again, his chest had a fine sheen of sweat on it and he was breathing like a mistreated racehorse. Getting his shirt on took another long, painful moment, during which time Nicole watch the tattooed design on his bicep bunch as he struggled. She bit her lip and clenched her fists to keep from helping.

And then he was heading toward the door.

"Ty—" When he looked at her impatiently, she sighed. "You can't drive on those painkillers I gave you."

"I didn't take the last two."

"You didn't—" She shook her head, understanding now why he was hurting so badly. "You really are a fool."

"No shit, doc." He had his computer tucked against his good side, and was half out the door, but he hesitated. "Thanks."

"For what? Pissing you off?"

Now he sighed. "For being there."

"Okay."

Crystal-blue haunted eyes watched warily as she walked up to him. When she got close enough, he closed his eyes, sighed again, then looked at her as he reached out and stroked her jaw. "I have to go," he whispered, running a finger up the hoops in her ear.

She barely resisted the urge to turn her face into his hand and kiss his palm. "Tell me why."

"Because I'm not fit for company." He stepped back and dropped his hand.

"Sometimes, Ty, you *have* to let people in."

"You're speaking from experience, of course."

She ignored the sarcasm. "I let my family in. And Suzanne and Taylor." *And you*, she wanted say. Horrifying, how much she wanted to say it, how much she wanted *him* to want it as well.

"Goodbye, Nicole."

"Wait.... You're not going to even write her back?"

"Do you really care?"

"You know I do."

"Actually, I know no such thing."

"How can you say that after last night?"

"We're different, you've said so enough times."

"Maybe those differences are more surface than I thought," she admitted.

"Meaning?"

"Meaning...we're both loners. We're both workaholics. Maybe we connect on a more fundamental level than I imagined possible."

"You're a doctor. Your own words, remember? I was hurt and you're sworn to heal. You would have done the same for a puppy."

She swallowed hard at her own words thrown back in her face and looked right at him, the hardest thing she'd ever done. "I care about you."

"Yeah, well, you shouldn't. Goodbye, Nicole."

And then he was gone, and she was staring at the closed door thinking that his goodbye had sounded a lot more final than just see-you-later.

It sounded like...well, goodbye.

And really, that was perfectly fine with her. More than fine.

Which didn't explain the tear on her cheek.

ONCE HE GOT home, Ty slept for two days straight. Then he lay around for a third and fourth in a funk that was very unlike him.

It was too quiet. That had to be why he thought of Nicole only every living second. To combat that, he cranked up the music. Watched TV. Worked.

But still, he thought of her. How could he not? She was smart and sexy and beautiful, and he wanted her. Yet he'd wanted plenty of women before, so why he felt so down about how he'd left her, he had no idea. They didn't have anything going, she didn't want to have anything going.

Neither did he. Yeah, he would have loved to sleep with her, hold her, sink into her body and lose himself, sating this inexplicable desire for her. But he hadn't, and it was over. He'd never been one to wonder about might-have-beens.

And yet he wondered now. Ironic that in his life, he'd had no patience for people who hesitated. Fate and destiny were out there to be taken advantage of, not to sit around and accept. He'd taken charge of his destiny, and because of it he had a great life. And if once in a while it was too...quiet, then he took care of it. It had never been difficult to find a woman interested in a good time, short-term of course. Maybe that's what he needed now. A bout of mutually satisfying, hot, sweaty sex.

Too bad he could hardly move.

Five days after falling through the ceiling, he drove by the youth hostel. Just out of curiosity, he told himself, not because of a strange sense that he was missing something, something important. He got out of his car and asked the young tattooed kid at the desk for Margaret Mary. He waited for what seemed like forever, his heart pounding uncomfortably against the ribs that still hurt, only to be told she wasn't around.

Good. Fine. It had been stupid to try to see her anyway. He didn't need to add trouble to his life, and family would be trouble.

Since he was out, he went by some of his jobs, ignoring his aching ribs, burying himself in the stuff he'd neglected over the past few days. By the time he got home, he was suitably exhausted. Dizzy with it, in fact. Maybe now, finally, he could sleep.

But at midnight he was still staring at the ceiling of his bedroom. He probably should have given in and taken some painkillers, but he hated the loss of control so he gritted his teeth and told himself he'd feel better tomorrow. Deciding to work, he flipped on a light, but the lines on the plans blurred and jumped around, making him feel nauseous.

Time for oblivion, he thought, and reached for the bottle of pills. But a knock at the door stopped him. Since he couldn't think of a single reason for someone to be knocking at his door at midnight, he ignored it.

It came again.

Struggling into a pair of sweat pants, he figured that since he didn't feel like crying as he moved, he must be improving. Still, by the time he hobbled to the door, he was ready to sit down. And when he opened it, he nearly *did* sit down, right there on the floor. "Nicole!"

She stood there, arms braced on the jamb on either side of her, head down. When he said her name, she lifted her face. Her short, dark hair was up in spikes, as if she'd shoved her fingers through it repeatedly. She wore a spaghetti-strapped tank top under overalls. One strap had slid down her shoulder. Her smooth, sleek arms were taut, her tight little body quivering with tension.

But it was her eyes that held him now, as they were filled with so many things it hurt to look at her.

"I woke you," she said. "I'm sorry, I'll just—"

He wrapped his fingers around her arm to stop her from backing away. Skin to skin. The jolt nearly brought him to his knees. Now was a hell of a time to realize that with her standing right here in front of him everything suddenly felt good. Right.

He hated that. She was nothing but a damn string on the heart he didn't want to feel.

"I shouldn't have come," she whispered.

No, no she shouldn't have. Because now he didn't know how to let her go.

"I just...I saw your light." She lifted a shoulder, gave him a little smile.

The smile lifted him in a way it shouldn't, and just like that, the funk was gone.

He'd have to dwell on that later because right now he wanted the feel of her. Needed the feel of her in a terrifyingly bad way.

"It's just that Taylor said she hadn't seen or heard from you," she said. "And you didn't make your check-up appointment the hospital gave you, and—"

With a little tug, he had her inside.

"So I just drove by, just to see...and well." She smiled again, stopping his heart. "Like I said, I saw the light—"

He shut the door behind her. She took one step back, away from him, right up against the wood.

Perfect.

"So." Her smile shook a bit now. "I just wanted to see for myself that you were doing okay—" She stopped when he planted an arm on either side of her head. "Are you going to say something?" she whispered, licking her bottom lip.

Oh yeah, he liked that little nervous gesture.

"Ty?"

"You want to give me a check-up?"

"I...uh..."

He found his own smile. "You're nervous, doc. I know it sounds sick, but I like that. I like that a lot."

She pressed her fingers to her eyes, which gave him better room to crowd her body.

So he did.

"You know what?" she murmured, still covering her eyes. "I'm going now." Then she dropped her hands and shoved at his chest, which shot a white-hot arrow of pain right through his ribs. Doubling over, he groaned, vaguely aware of her horrified gasp.

"Oh, Ty—" Her hands came around his bare middle.

"Damn it—"

"I know, I know, I'm so sorry."

He sucked in a careful breath and looked at her when she said it again. Her hands on his skin moved lightly, not a doctor's hands, but a woman's, as she murmured her apologies over and over, as she tried to soothe. And little by little his vision cleared so that he could straighten slightly.

"Are you okay?" she whispered.

"I'll let you know when the stars clear from my head."

"God. I'm so sorry."

"I know."

"I...wouldn't hurt you on purpose."

"I know."

But she already had. Nicole could feel it. She just didn't understand. *He* was the one who didn't want a relationship. *He* was the one who'd kept her at arm's length with his light, easygoing, teasing attitude. He was the one...

Wasn't he?

"Nicole." That was it, that was the only word to escape his lips, but his gaze seemed to say so much more. Eyes hot, he lowered his head so that their lips were only a breath apart. "Why did you come?"

She licked her lips again. "I told you, I—"

"*Why*, Nicole?"

She closed her eyes, trying to hide the truth from

him. She'd come to be in his arms. She'd come to give him what she'd held back all this time. She'd come to see if she was going crazy, or if this...this thing went both ways.

"Nicole?"

"Y-yes?"

"I should tell you, watching you struggle at this social stuff is an incredible turn-on. Knowing you're usually buried in work, that you never look up from that work for anyone, and you are now...because of me..."

She stared down at his hand as it entwined with hers and tugged. Then she was staring at his strong, sleekly muscled back while he led her through the house.

"I'm taking you to my bedroom now," he said over his shoulder. "Stop me."

She kept following him.

He tugged her into a room lit only by the moonlight dancing through the wall of windows. Then he flipped on the light and she was blinking at him like an owl.

"I want to see this." He stepped so close she could see nothing but him. Around her, she had an impression of a large room, an equally large bed with tossed blankets and sheets.

Then he backed her to that bed, his eyes glowing with intent and emotion. "I think you came for this, which just so happens to be what I'm looking for as well."

"You— But you're hurt." Since when did she stutter? The mattress bumped her high on the back of her thighs. Her heart was drumming so fast and so loud it was a wonder he hadn't asked her if she was having a heart attack.

"Say I'm wrong." He lifted a finger and nudged off the other strap of her overalls. The bib fell to her waist, leaving just her thin tank top, which hid nothing from him, including the fact she was aroused. Very aroused.

His head dipped, and for a long moment he just looked, making her nipples tighten and pucker against the thin material all the more. "Nicole." His voice was husky. "You're not saying no."

"I—"

"No starts with N." He used both hands now, gliding his fingers up and down her arms. He met her gaze. Waited.

She licked her lips, which wrestled a low groan from him. And then he leaned in even closer. "Say it. Say no."

"I don't want to say it." Almost before she'd finished, his mouth closed over hers. She opened to him and he groaned again. Then he was inside, tasting her as if he was a starving man and she was a ten-course meal. Which worked for her because suddenly, or maybe not so suddenly, she was starving too, starving for this.

Breaking only for air, he raised his head and stared at her from slumberous eyes before he came at her again, changing the angle of the kiss, settling his mouth more firmly over hers. Her lips clung to his as her fingers fisted in his hair, holding him to the plundering, caressing kiss because she didn't want him pulling back again. She wanted this mindlessness, craved this hot, sensual heat, and needed even more.

They broke apart for air again, and stared at each other. His hands lifted to untangle her arms from around his neck. He danced his fingers back up, wrapping them around her spaghetti straps. Still holding her gaze in his, he gave a hard tug, peeling the material down to her waist, exposing her bare breasts.

Dropping his gaze, his chest rose and fell with his uneven breathing as he looked at the breasts she knew damn well were too small. Thinking it, she lifted her hands but he caught them, held them at her sides.

"Are you saying no?" he asked thickly.

"Ty—"

"Are you?"

His eyes were fathomless, his body tense. Against her belly she could feel him, hard and pulsing. He wanted her. He wanted her in a way she hadn't been wanted in too long. "I'm not saying no," she said softly.

The tension left him in a long sigh. "Thank God," he murmured, and let go of her wrists to cup her breasts. "You're beautiful."

And in that moment, she felt it.

"And these..." His thumbs rasped over her nipples, making her let out a horrifyingly needy sound. "Oh yeah, these..." Bending his head, he swirled his tongue over one, then blew a soft, warm breath over it, forcing that sound from her again. "Mmm. A perfect mouthful." Proving the point, he sucked her into his mouth, laving her with his tongue over and over until she'd refisted her hands in his hair and tossed back her head, panting for air.

It wasn't enough. Kicking off her shoes made her even shorter but she didn't care. Rising up on the balls of her feet, she hooked a leg over his hips and strained against the swollen ridge of his erection.

That ripped a deep, deep groan of pleasure from his chest and he pulled back to look at her with eyes heavy with desire. "Last chance."

She tugged at the tie of his sweats, making him let out a laughing moan. "Okay, so you don't want a last chance." With a not-so-gentle shove, he pushed her backwards, tumbling her to the mattress. He put a knee on the bed and grabbed the hem of her overalls. Looked at her. Pulled. Tossing them over his shoulder, he did the same with her tank top, leaving her in just a light-blue silky thong.

"Now." His other knee hit the bed. Towering over her, he looked down and let out a smile that made her swallow hard. "Let's discuss this lingerie thing you have going." With one finger he traced the silk down her hip, over her mound, stopping just shy of the spot that would make her a complete wanton.

"I— It's—"

"And this stuttering thing. That's new." His smile was tight and just a bit intimidating as he hooked a finger in the panties and whipped them off.

"You're overdressed," she managed to say when he just looked down at her, his eyes shining like crystal and very intense.

"Yeah. About that." On his knees leaning over her, he'd gone utterly still. "I should tell you, I can't move."

"Oh, Ty!" Scampering up to her knees, she faced him, putting her hands on his bare, hot, deliciously hard chest. "I'm sorry, I—"

He put a finger to her lips. "Don't even think about being sorry or turning back into a doctor." Very slowly, very carefully, he lay down on his back. Then let out a slow breath.

"Okay?" she asked, leaning over him now, their positions reversed.

Lifting his hands, he cupped the breasts that were

in his face. "Very okay." Raising his head, he replaced his fingers with his tongue, leaving his hands free to skim down her spine, down the backs of her thighs, which he urged open. Grabbing one leg, he pulled, so that she fell over his chest, straddling him.

She was careful to brace herself high, on his pecs, rather than press on his ribs. "Still okay?"

His hands glided up her legs, her hips, her waist, cupping and squeezing her breasts before sliding down the quivering muscles of her stomach. "So damn okay." His hands met over her belly button, and his thumbs danced down, down, until they slid into the curls at the apex of her thighs.

"Ty—"

"Oh yeah. Love it when you say my name like that. Like you're hot and shaky and on the edge. On the edge for me."

She was. Hot and shaky and on the edge. For him. She ached with it, ached with the desire and emptiness and the need for him to fill her up.

"I've wanted you since that first moment I saw you," he said, sinking his thumbs lower, making her gasp. "Say you want me back."

She cried out when he gave one long, slow, sure stroke of his thumb right where she needed it. "I want you."

"Then take me. Take us both the hell away." His voice was rough, and when she lifted up, yanked down his sweats and came right back on him, gliding hot, damp skin to hot, damp skin, he groaned.

"Nicole—" He tried to surge up, hurt himself, and let out a pained, frustrated growl.

"Shh." She pressed him back. "Let me—"

"Yes."

"Don't move."

"I won't if you will," he swore, and their next kiss was an avaricious feeding frenzy of mouth and teeth and tongues and wordless murmurs and demands, while their hands tore at each other. She stroked his chest, then ran her fingers down his belly to wrap a fist around the hot, velvety steel of him, while he did something magical with his fingers, leaving her a gasping, panting mass of nerve endings. The tension inside her built and pulled and made her crazy, more so when he rubbed his straining erection back and forth over her exposed, swollen flesh.

"Condom," he said through gritted teeth. "Night-stand."

"Got it." She tore it open, straddled him again. Took him in her hands and protected them both. Then he took over, guiding her over him so that he brushed against her slick opening. Gripping her hips, pulling her down as he thrust up, he slid home, stretching her, filling her to the hilt.

The sensation of having him inside her was so powerful, so...complete, she sobbed out his name and fell over him to meet his mouth with hers. His grip on her hips tightened, and he lifted her almost entirely off him before plunging her downward again, harder.

"Oh, my— *Ty.*"

"I know." His head fell back and his powerful body quivered beneath hers. "I know."

Her legs tightened at his hips as she lifted herself back up, slowly moving him in and out of her body in a delicious, sensual ride, going faster, then faster still as the pressure built. Her pulse beat in her throat, her breath soughed in and out of her lungs as they hammered each other, over and over. Nothing had ever felt like this, no one had ever made her feel like this, as if she was home right there in his arms. Each thrust, each flex of his hips brought her closer, and then he tugged her down and put his mouth to a breast.

She exploded, and like the entire frenzied mating, there was nothing easy or slow about it. Shudder upon shudder shook her body, rippling across her flesh, until she was nothing but an exposed nerve ending, weightless and helpless as what felt like a train wreck occurred in her head, her heart, her soul.

Vaguely, from far, far away, she heard Ty cry out, too, felt him go rigid beneath her as he found his own release. His fingers dug into her hips as he pumped into her body, hard, one last time.

Seeing him, hearing him while he sought his pleasure, unbelievably triggered yet another tremor within her, and her body arched mindlessly into his as she lost herself again.

The next thing she felt were his strong, warm arms pulling her down, turning them both, so they lay face-to-face, limbs entangled. His heart hammered against her cheek while she continued to try to catch her breath. She couldn't. She felt battered, bruised and yet so wildly euphoric she was surprised she wasn't floating high in the air.

Oh yeah, she was at home here in his arms, and given how relaxed Ty felt next to her, he felt at home, too. And just like that, for the first time in Nicole's entire adult life, she felt good at something other than work.

10

WARM AND SATED, Nicole opened her eyes and found Ty watching her through his own half-opened baby blues.

He was so beautiful. It wasn't often she needed a physical release, which meant it wasn't often she'd had recreational sex. But this...this had been nothing like her previous sexual encounters.

First of all, she'd had an orgasm. Easily. Almost from just looking at him. Second, she'd nearly wept at the intensity of it.

And third, she wanted to do it again.

But Ty didn't utter a single word. He didn't have to, as with each passing second, his gaze grew more pained, more exhausted.

And more guarded.

"Go to sleep," she whispered, a weariness replacing her pathetic, and it seemed, premature, joy.

His lids fell shut. Without a word.

And when he was out like a light, she left.

Without a word.

TY WASN'T SURPRISED when he awoke alone, but damn, he had to admit to feeling disappointment. If he was smart, he'd attribute that to the morning hard-on that wouldn't quit even after a gut-sucking cold shower. But even he knew enough to admit his problem wasn't physical.

Before he could give too much thought to the matter, he called Nicole at home. What he planned on saying, he hadn't a clue. *Hey. Good orgasm, huh?* Or, *Why did you leave? I wanted to get laid again.*

Maybe he should stick with the truth. *I woke up reaching for you and when I found you gone I was lonely as hell.*

But in the end, he said nothing because he got her answering machine and hung up. She'd left without a word, and he should have the grace to accept that. Last night had been nothing more complicated than two adults taking care of their needs.

He just hoped he got to take care of her needs again soon.

He went about his day, somewhat heartened that he didn't feel like throwing up every time he moved. And then there was the fact his entire body hummed with the remembered vibrations of spectacular sex.

And it *had* been spectacular. Fireworks, earthquake, the entire enchilada.

Not that he hadn't had really spectacular sex before, but...ah, hell. He'd never had really spectacular sex before. Not like that anyway, where he'd really, truly lost control, giving everything he had over to a woman, keeping his eyes open when he came so that he could see into hers, and feel her heart and soul while she did the same.

Scary stuff.

Work helped a little, as he was swamped. And when he went by Taylor's building to discuss the plans with her, he told himself he would just peek in on Nicole.

Just to say hey.

Naturally, she was at work. Most likely not even thinking about him.

Taylor and Suzanne plied him with food and laughter. It felt good, which was strange. Normally such a thing would smother him. After all, he hadn't even slept with either of them and they wanted to spoil him and talk to him and...be friends.

It wasn't often he'd been friends with a woman, much less two of them, but resisting either Taylor or Suzanne was pretty much impossible.

Plus, he liked them, at least until he was reminded that the engagement party was that night and as their friend, he was expected to attend.

Two more strings on his heart.

And seeing as he had those strings, he figured he might as well go all the way. Once again, he drove to the youth hostel and asked for Margaret Mary.

And once again was told sorry. Only this time, he

was sorry, too. She'd moved out, moved on, he was told.

Ty gripped the front desk and wondered at the drop in his stomach. "Moved on to where?"

The young kid shrugged. "I think she said she was interested in seeing Seattle."

Seattle. One thousand miles away. Did she have a car? Did she have money? Or was she out there, all alone, no means and no friends, and too young to know danger when she looked it in the face?

Ty had no idea what his sudden rush was, but he raced home for his e-mail.

Nothing. No long, windy messages from her, no short appealing messages from her, nothing.

What did that mean? Had she given up on him? It wouldn't surprise him, as he deserved exactly that.

For the first time, *he* initiated contact.

Margaret Mary of Dublin,

I am Irish and I am stubborn and I am sorry. I know this is nothing but a lousy excuse, but please try to understand. Family has never given me anything but pain and suffering.

But I have the feeling you would have been different. I don't know what changed my mind, whether it was the fall on my head (long story) or the fact that I woke up alone this morning and knew I'd done that to myself (another long story).

So Margaret Mary of Dublin, am I too late?

Ty Patrick O'Grady, your brother.

Leaning back in his chair, Ty looked out of his great big picture window at the San Gabriel Mountains. What a glorious view this huge house gave him.

This huge, *empty* house.

When had that happened? When had the house become too big, too quiet? There had been a time when that's all he'd wanted, his own space and quiet.

But now, he needed...more. What, exactly, he wasn't certain.

But definitely, things were missing. And, if he was admitting such things, people.

He was missing people.

NICOLE MANAGED, with a good amount of swearing and disgust, to get herself ready for the engagement party that night. She also managed to avoid Taylor and her bag of makeup and hair stuff by staying late at work, because nylons, a fancy dress, mascara and a dab of gloss was as good as she was going to give.

The party was taking place at Ryan's house, which Suzanne was moving in to. The moment Nicole walked in, she was assaulted by the scent of delicious food—thank God—and music and laughter.

And hugs. Everyone wanted to hug her. Suzanne. Taylor. Ryan. She pushed away Suzanne and Taylor because they were hooting and hollering at her in the dress, and let Ryan in for a good long hug.

"Hey, that's my almost-husband," Suzanne protested when Ryan, tall, dark and gorgeous, hugged Nicole back.

"Just being sisterly," Nicole said, and gave Ryan a smacking kiss on the lips, enjoying Suzanne's hiss and Taylor's laugh.

Then another man walked up to them. He was tall, dark and gorgeous too, more so, if that was even possible, with sharp blue eyes, a sometime-Irish accent and attitude to match hers.

"Hey," she said, a little defiantly, but damn it, she suddenly felt...conspicuous.

That Ty's gaze nearly gobbled her up from head to toe and all the spots in between didn't help. "Hey, yourself," he said.

Suzanne pulled Taylor and Ryan away with a completely obvious and annoying wink.

Leaving her alone with Ty. Unable to stand still, she shifted on the stupid heels, nibbled off her gloss. Before she could stop herself, she tugged at the hem of her dress. Damn, she felt stupid. Exposed.

Ty stepped closer, and she shifted again, feeling the need to smack him. Kiss him. If only she was dressed in jeans.

Then Ty put a hand on her waist and squeezed gently. "You steal my heart."

Ah, hell. When he said shit like that, her heart just tipped right on its side. "Stop it."

"It's true. You're amazing."

"A pair of heels and a ridiculous dress make me amazing?"

"No, your heart makes you amazing," he said softly, and stroked her jaw. "You got all dressed up for Suzanne. You love her."

"I knew she'd have good food."

He shook his head. "Play tough if you need to, I see right through you."

Yeah. He did, he saw right through her.

Terrifying.

NICOLE'S PLAN was to stay busy at work. That way she didn't have to think about Ty. The way he'd looked so good at the engagement party she'd wanted to gobble him up whole. The way he'd whispered those hot, sexy words in her ear as he held her close, which was every moment. The way his intense eyes had promised her the world even as he let her go home—alone.

She managed to use work to keep her busy for small periods of time, but Ty was proving to be hard to forget. One day the following week she stood studying a patient's chart in the nearly deserted nurses' station, lost in her own world.

Until Dr. Watts came up behind her. "You smell good," he whispered, standing inappropriately close. So close in fact, that the front of his thighs brushed the backs of hers.

"Back up," she warned. He had her pinned between the counter and his body, but she was far more pissed than worried. She could drop him to the floor in an instant; she just didn't want the scene that would follow.

"Why do you resist me?" he asked, his fingers stroking her neck.

She slapped his hand away. "I'm going to tell you one more time. Keep your paws off me."

"Or what?"

"Or you'll be sorry. Now back off."

His soft laughter was her only answer; he still stood in her space. Then he brushed his hips to hers and she saw red.

"You feel good—" he started to say, but ended on a whoosh of a breath when she plowed her elbow into his belly and stomped on his foot hard enough to drop him to the floor like a log.

"Well, then."

With a sigh, she shoved her hair out of her eyes, turned around to face the new male voice, and came face-to-face with Dr. Luke Walker.

Medical chair. The man in charge of just about anything there was to be in charge of, including Dr. Lincoln Watts, writhing on the floor. "Problem, Dr.
Mann?" he asked over Linc's body.

"Not any more."

He eyed the man on the floor, then looked her over
carefully before he said quietly, "You should have
come to me sooner, Nicole."

She let out a slow breath. "I'm fine."

"Good, then. Please, consider your shift over."

"But—"

"Not as a punishment." He stepped back as Dr.
Watts struggled to his feet. "Consider it a small pay-
ment for your patience with the system. Dr. Watts,
come with me, please."

Linc shot Nicole a look to kill, and she had to turn
away to hide her grin. In fact, she grinned all the way
to her car, then sang all the way home through South
Village traffic, and actually got a great parking spot
right out front before she remembered she didn't really want to go home.

She climbed the steps to the building thinking she
should have stopped for some take-out, but before
she could let herself in, Suzanne was there, smiling at
her.

Nicole scrunched her forehead, trying to remember. "Did I miss a wedding planning session?"

"Nope. I just wanted to say hello."

"Me, too, you twit." Taylor slung an arm around Suzanne's shoulders and looked at Nicole. "You ever heard of returning phone calls?"

She'd gotten their messages but hadn't had the time to get back to them. Now that she was looking into their relaxed, happy-to-see-her faces, guilt sank in. Why hadn't she made the time? "See, this is why I don't do the friendship thing." She unlocked her door and gestured them in. "I'm terrible at it."

"You're not, you're just busy."

"But you do have to remember we exist," Taylor told her. "That would be nice."

"I'm sorry. Work—"

"Yeah, yeah." Taylor put her hands on her hips and studied the ceiling she'd had patched. "I don't suppose you even noticed I had this fixed."

In truth, she hadn't. What did that say about her? Besides the fact she'd purposely been so busy she hadn't had time to breathe? "Um..."

"Rhetorical question," Taylor assured her. "Don't hurt yourself."

"Look, I have to—"

"You just got home from work, what could you possibly have to do?" Taylor sank into the futon couch in the living room and looked around. "You need furniture in a bad way."

"Yeah."

"That's a pretty noncommittal yeah. You planning

on moving soon? Is that why you've never settled in here?"

"I've settled in. I have a bed."

"Uh-huh." Taylor lifted an eyebrow. "And half your kitchen is still in boxes on the floor."

"That's because Suzanne keeps bringing me food so I haven't had to cook." Nicole smiled at Suzanne. "Thanks, by the way."

Suzanne smiled back. "Should I stop? Would that make you stay? If you had to settle in here?"

"Stay? But..." She looked back and forth between them. "I'm not going anywhere."

"You sure about that?" Taylor stood, came closer. "Because I still have your rental app, which clearly states you haven't stayed in one place for longer than a few months. We're coming up on that mark now. Is it nearly time to move on? You've got a few people who care here, and I can tell it's unnerving you." She nodded as she studied Nicole far too closely. "Yeah," she murmured. "Nearly time to move on, isn't it?"

Nicole crossed her arms. "So I haven't lived in one spot for long, so what? Lots of people suffer from wanderlust and besides, I've had my job for a good long while, and that's not going to change. That's got to count as stability."

Suzanne's smile was sad. "I don't think it's really wanderlust affecting you, Nicole. I think it's fear of letting people close. I know, because before I met and fell in love with Ryan, I was the same way. Never really let people in."

Nicole turned to Taylor. "We have a vow of single-hood, have you forgotten? I'm pretty certain that means never letting people in."

"It means you don't put a diamond on the ring finger of your left hand. But you sure as hell can do just about everything else, and should." Taylor tipped her head to the side and studied Nicole until she squirmed. "You know we love you, right? And I think you feel something for us back."

"Well, mostly for Suzanne because she cooks for me," Nicole said, trying to tease past the sudden lump in her throat. She never quite knew what to do with emotion, with easy affection such as she was being offered.

"And I know you feel something for Ty—"

"Actually, what I feel mostly right now is irritation."

Taylor lifted a brow. "Are you saying you don't like him?"

"Well, I—"

"It was all over your face when he got hurt, Nicole."

"Because I'm a doctor! I hate to see *anyone* hurt, including a know-it-all Irishman."

"You were beside yourself because it *was* the know-it-all Irishman," Taylor pointed out. "So much so that you even forgot your training. That was huge, you panicking like that. Huge and very unlike you."

"You even took a day off," Suzanne so helpfully reminded her. "Remember?"

"How could she forget?" Taylor grinned. "She discovered soap operas and cheesy old classic reruns. And she allowed herself to feel, to care. Didn't you, Nicole?"

What Nicole remembered most was the simple pleasure of that day. Sitting, for a change. And yes, watching TV. But most of all, she remembered the sight of Ty in her bed. Remembered thinking she could get used to that.

"Or was it so good you scared yourself?" Suzanne asked quietly.

"You guys have far too much time to think, you know that?" Nicole hugged herself, feeling...naked. "Yes, I care. Okay? I care about a lot of stuff."

"How about Ty?"

"Yes, fine, Ty. Should I say it louder? *I care for Ty!* I care for him a lot." She lowered her voice to a soft sigh. "So much that it terrifies me, and diving back into work was all I had. Happy now?"

Ty stood in the front doorway, eyes on Nicole, smile grim. "I'm a lot of things, actually."

Nicole nearly swallowed her tongue. When the hell had he shown up? "Ty, I—"

"I don't have much experience with happy," he

continued. "But terrified?" He pondered that. "Definitely. I'm definitely terrified, Nicole."

Suzanne put her hand on his arm and gave him a gentle squeeze. "It gets easier."

"What does?"

"Why, love of course." She smiled into his shocked face and reached for Taylor. "We'll just leave the two of you alone—"

"No!" Nicole softened her voice with effort. Her heart was pounding. Her palms damp. She wanted to start running like hell and never stop. Love? Who'd said anything about love? For God's sake, couldn't one lust for someone without the L-word coming into play? "Taylor—"

Taylor just laughed at Nicole's face. "Oh, sweetie, if you could see your expression. Well, girlfriend, you've been too busy for too long, you never learned to slow down and take it all in. Now it's happened without your permission, hasn't it? And you haven't a clue what to do with it. Poor baby." She grabbed Nicole's face and gave her a smacking kiss. "Good news, Super Girl. You're smart, you'll figure it out."

Okay, maybe Nicole had only recently realized what she was missing in her life. Maybe she'd only recently understood that life wasn't all work and no play, but she still hadn't reconciled it all, she still didn't know how to get more for herself, or how to...

How to face Ty, the man she'd foolishly thought maybe, possibly, hopefully could be the one.

He *wasn't* the one. He wouldn't ever want to be the one.

And he'd heard her shout how she felt about him. God. Talk about humiliation. "Taylor—"

But they were gone. Leaving her alone with Ty, who was looking at her with an expression she supposed mirrored her own terror. "Well." She tried to smile. "My day is complete."

He blew out a breath and looked at her. Really looked at her. "Something else is wrong," he said.

"Besides you being here?"

"What is it?"

"Nothing," she muttered, a little cross that he could see through everything and find the lingering unease over the Dr. Watts scene. "It's just that work sucked and now—"

"Did that asshole try something again?"

She stared at him, a little shocked by his deep tone of instant rage. For her. "Everything is going to be fine in that department."

"Sure?"

His voice was every bit as low and gravely and sexy as she remembered, and she remembered plenty. "Very."

He drew another deep breath as if struggling for patience.

She knew the feeling. "So why are you here anyway?" she asked, more than a little defensively, crossing her arms.

"I have a job here."

"Oh, yeah." Now she felt just stupid. Of course he had a job here. What did she think, that he'd come to see her? How ridiculous that would be, how—

"I'll just get to it," he said, and turned to the door.

Only he slammed it shut while still on the inside, closing them inside the apartment together.

Alone.

11

TY LOOKED at Nicole, who stood there seeming a little confused.

Good, that made two of them.

"What are you doing?" she asked warily when he came close. "I thought you were going to go do what you had to."

"I am." He wrapped his hands around her upper arms and hauled her up to her toes so he could get a good look into the face he couldn't seem to stop thinking about.

She gasped. "But...I thought you meant work. You had to get to work."

"Who said anything about work?"

"You—I—"

"There you go stuttering again." He set her down but didn't take his hands off her. "I'm beginning to think you only do that around me, and you know what? I like it. But let's stick to the subject. I want to set the record straight between us."

"Oh." Her face cleared of all expression. She was good at that, he'd noticed, but then again, so was he.

"I see," she said stiffly.

"I doubt it."

"No, I do. You regret what happened between us."

"Is that what you think?" He tipped up her face and saw that was exactly what she thought. "Is that why you left my bed?"

"Don't tell me you wanted to wake up with me." She pulled her chin free of his fingers. "I saw the look in your eyes before you fell asleep. Panic, pure and simple."

"What you saw was fleeting."

"Because you fell asleep." She closed her eyes. "And I didn't blame you for it, so don't worry. I'm not the kind of woman a man wants to wake up with."

He swore, then shoved his fingers through his hair and turned in a slow circle, trying to find the words. "Nicole, you're *exactly* the kind of woman a man wants to wake up with. You're smart, and sexy as hell. You're *amazing*. But I was lying there, holding you, still shaking like a leaf, damn it, from the most incredible..." He let out a disparaging sound, having no idea how to say it. "Look, what we shared was different. First of all, I've never come so hard in my life."

She blushed, her expression one of surprise.

"But it wasn't just sex," he said. "I know that sounds like a line, but it wasn't. What we shared was a connection, a real one, and yes, damn it, it scared the living daylights out of me."

She was very still. "Go on."

Go on. Hell. He licked his suddenly dry lips. "I felt closer to you than I have to anyone. Ever."

The fist around her heart, the one that had been there since she'd first set eyes on him, loosened slightly. "Really?"

"I felt like you knew me."

A warmth spread through her. "I did. I do. Ty, I do."

"No." Now he closed his eyes. "You don't understand." He turned away, his shoulders stiff. "I came from nothing, Nicole. I was nothing."

"No, never that." Her heart ached that he pictured himself that way.

"You have no idea some of the things I did to survive."

"No one would ever blame the child you were," she said fiercely. "No one. And you shouldn't either."

"I know." Misery radiated off him, so that she was propelled forward, propelled to put her hand on his back. His muscles leapt at her touch.

"But I'm still that boy deep inside," he admitted. "I'm still that wanderer. I still feel that need to keep moving. I...I started to feel that need again."

Now her heart all but stopped as he turned back to look at her.

"You...you're moving on?" she asked.

"I've thought about it. Then I heard from my sister and I *really* thought about it." There was nothing but truth in his eyes, the man who'd taught her the one thing no one else had ever managed, how to live outside the box. He was strong and smart and made her smile. He was passionate about work, about life, about everything in between. And unlike anyone before him, he made her feel the same way back.

"It'd be so easy," he said. "Easy to pick up and go start over." He lifted a shoulder. "New York sounded good."

"Yeah." She cleared her throat because it was so thick. He'd thought about leaving, walking away. "Ty..." *Don't. Don't go.*

Reaching out, he ran his fingers over her jaw. Slid them down her throat and cupped the back of her head, tugging her a step closer. Mouth close to hers, his turned down in a grim, unbearably sad smile, he said, "But then I met you."

He still looked so utterly intent on going that there was no logical reason why hope suddenly burned through her bright as the sun. "And...?"

"And...for the first time I wanted someone to know about me, know my past. Accept it. We know we're different, Nicole. That I—"

She stopped him with her mouth on his. She knew his past shamed him. Just as she knew the man he really was, a man with a heart and soul dying for acceptance and love, just like anyone else. He could hold people off with his easy charm and laid-back attitude, but he couldn't hold her off, not for another second.

He tried. Despite her mouth clinging to his, despite her arms wound around his neck, he hadn't touched her, not yet, so she pulled back and held his face in her hands. "Please want me, too, Ty, if only half as much as I want you."

"Half?" He let out a half growl, half laugh. "*Half.* Hell..."

"It's okay, I—"

"I want you more than my next breath, damn it." His arms came around her hard, lifting her up against him. "But you're supposed to know what's good for you. Nicole, you're supposed to send me away. You're supposed to stay away from me."

"I won't. I can't."

"Well, then God help the both of us." His mouth came down on hers again, but he shocked her with unexpected tenderness, with an irresistible gentleness, coaxing and nibbling her into a hunger only he could sate.

As if she needed coaxing. After a long, wet, hot kiss, he lifted his head and stared at her. The hunger must have been all over her face because he groaned, and then his mouth slashed across hers again, and this time when they tore apart for air, they stared wild and wide-eyed at each other.

"Not here," she said breathlessly, staggering when he pulled back. "My bed."

"Nicole—"

"My bed," she repeated, and grabbed his hand, tugging him toward her bedroom before he could come to his senses and say goodbye. She didn't want goodbyes, and she was banking on the hope he didn't really want them either.

It was late and the room was dark. She flipped on the light switch, then hesitated. Maybe she should leave them in the dark, give them some place to hide.

No. *No*, she thought, turning back to him as she pulled her shirt over her head and watched his gaze flare with unchecked desire. She wanted to see him want her. Wanted to capture that and save it. Store it in a part of her heart to pull out when she needed.

After he was gone.

"Nicole—"

She wanted to cry at the rough, low voice, tinged with regret. He wasn't going to change his mind, not now, he couldn't. She unbuttoned her jeans and he swallowed hard.

"Wait, I—" His words broke off into a rough groan when she shoved the jeans down her hips and kicked them free, leaving her in a siren-red lace bra and a sunshine-yellow silk thong. Laundry day, damn it.

She never matched for him. But she couldn't worry about that now. To make sure he saw her, all of her, she turned in a slow circle, running her hands down her own body.

When she turned back to him, he was suddenly right there, so close she bumped into his chest. "Not fair," he whispered.

"What's not fair is that you haven't started." She tugged on his shirt. He raised his arms so that she could pull it off and toss it over her shoulder. The bruises on his ribs made her physically ache for him. "Are you okay?"

"Right now I am. I love your color choices today."

She grimaced. "One of these days I'll get it together and pay attention in the morning."

"No, I like it. Tough, cool tomboy on the outside, thoroughly unorganized siren on the inside." His palms slid up her sides to cup her breasts, while she combed her fingers through his hair, bringing his mouth back to hers for the hot, wet, deep kiss she'd been longing for.

"Nicole." His voice was hoarse, and he repeated her name as if he couldn't hear it enough. He kissed her jaw, beneath her ear, her throat, touching her everywhere his hands could reach. Then her bra fell to the floor, followed by her mismatched panties. "I don't want to hurt you," he said.

"Then don't." She opened his jeans and slid her

hands inside, squeezing his very squeezable butt. Not enough, but she knew he couldn't easily bend so she dropped to her knees to work his jeans down. She tugged off his knit boxers, too, her mouth watering as his impressive erection sprang free.

"Nicole—"

She took him in her mouth and he staggered back a step, then swore reverently as his hands entangled in her hair. His head fell back. She ran her tongue up his length, and he shuddered, but then pulled away and hauled her up to her feet.

"Ty, I want to—"

"Bed. Now."

"But—"

"I'd play the hero and toss you on it," he said in a thrilling rough voice. "But—"

"Your ribs."

"My ribs," he agreed, following her down to the mattress. Lying at her side, he touched her feet, ran his hands up her calves, over her knees...then met her gaze as he wrapped his palm around her thigh.

"Careful of your ribs—" Her words ended abruptly when he splayed open her legs.

Staring down at her with such intense heat she felt herself go up in flames, he let out a slow breath. "I won't hurt myself, I won't have to. You're already killing me."

Very carefully, he shifted his weight. His intent became clear when she felt his warm breath high on her inner thigh. "Careful—"

"Shh." He kissed her quivering, slick flesh, and suddenly her skin felt tight, her chest too small to hold her heart. Then he kissed her again, and writhing on the sheets, she cried out.

"I want you." His gaze locked on her as he slid a finger into her body. Her moan of pleasure meshed with his. "I want you more than I've ever wanted anyone."

"I want you, too." She barely managed to put the words together, but sensed how much he needed to hear them to ground him here, to this place. To her. "I want you more than I've ever wanted anyone, Ty. Love me."

"Like this?" Sliding his hands beneath her, he put his mouth on her, and with one slow, sure, knowing stroke of his tongue he nearly drove her right out of her living mind. Then he sucked her into his mouth, and he *did* drive her right out of her living mind. While she was still trembling with the aftershocks, he came up to his knees, wrapped his hand around his erection and buried himself deep within her.

Then he went still as he uttered one concise and perfectly descriptive oath.

She was just about crazy with the need for him to move within her. *"What?"*

"Condom," he growled, and pulled out of her, his

sex glistening with her own wetness. She watched him grit his teeth as he got off the bed, searched out his wallet, opened a foil packet, and stroked a condom down the length of himself.

"Hurry," she said.

"This isn't the emergency room, Dr. Hot Pants. There's no hurry." And he proceeded to prove it to her by slowly, far too slowly, entering her again, watching her with hot, hot eyes as he did.

Oh, he destroyed her, completely destroyed her. Arching her hips, she tried to pull him in, faster, harder.

"Slow," he whispered, running hot, openmouthed kisses along her jaw, her throat, pulling a patch of her skin into his mouth to suck.

But she needed all of him and she needed it now. She needed that to ease her tight chest, to soothe her fear that she'd wake up and he'd be gone. "Ty—"

But he couldn't be rushed, so she slapped her hands to his tight butt and tugged. Still no go. He was a solid mass of muscle, with a mind of his own.

He held her like that, on the very edge. She would have been furious at the way he mastered her body if he hadn't been right there with her, head back, jaw clenched in a grimace of passion, just as on the edge as she. Then, when she was nearly sobbing in frustration, he thrust deep, stretching her, filling her. The penetration was so powerful and complete they both cried out, and then again when he withdrew only to plunge back in. His grip on her hips tightened as he stroked harder, deeper, his powerful body crushing her to the mattress.

Legs tightening around his waist, she moved with him, slowly at first, as he'd wanted, but the pressure built until her heart beat in her ears in tune to the thrust of his pumping hips.

Intense pleasure gripped her, shoved her over the edge as lights exploded behind her eyes and shudders rippled her body, robbing her of breath. Vaguely she felt him bury his face in her neck and groan out her name as he followed her over, but all she could do was cling to him, lost, as hot wave after hot wave continued to take her.

Ty collapsed to the side, hauling her with him. They lay still like that except for the sound of their racing hearts and uneven breathing.

Nicole concentrated on the physical, which was incredible, and refused to think of anything else. Then Ty kissed her shoulder and pulled back so he could look into her eyes. "Okay?"

"Definitely." She might have said fantastic. Euphoric. Better than she'd ever been. But he got out of the bed and disappeared into the bathroom.

She stared at the ceiling.

When he came back out, he stood by the bed, still

naked, looking down at her with those depthless eyes. "Should I go?"

Go? The thought made her heart clench. No. No, he shouldn't go. To show him, she lifted the covers, held them open.

He flipped off the light, climbed in, and scooped her close. She put her face into the crook of his neck, loving the feel of his warm, strong arms around her, having his hard body cradling hers as if he never wanted to let her go.

She loved him.

She knew that now, even though she'd never felt such an overwhelming, terrifying emotion for a man before. It was a bitter pill to swallow that Taylor, smug Taylor, had been right. The L-word *was* involved.

Now what? Good God, now what? *Deep breath, Nicole.* After all, she'd handled some pretty tough situations before, she could handle this.

They could handle this. Together.

That thought held her, made her smile in her sleep, made her smile as she woke up with the sun shining in her eyes.

She smiled all the way until she reached for Ty and found him gone.

12

HE COULDN'T REALLY be gone. Nicole cocked her head and listened, thinking he'd gotten in the shower, or was in the kitchen, though God knew, the fridge was so empty she couldn't imagine what was keeping him.

But, she heard nothing, and the truth hit her. Ty was gone and she was alone. No problem, really, as she was used to that, and she lay back in a relaxed pose to prove it.

But then she heard a sound in the hallway, and before she could think about it, she'd leapt from the bed so fast her head spun. Maybe he'd just gone for donuts and coffee.

If that was the case, she'd love him forever.

Hand on the front door, she realized she was still entirely naked so she went racing back into the bedroom, grabbed the blanket they'd tossed to the floor sometime in the deep, dark of the night when they hadn't needed anything but the heat they'd generated while making love.

Back at the front door, wrapped in the blanket now, she hauled the door open.

Nothing.

But since she still heard sounds, she tiptoed down a few stairs, thinking any moment now he'd pop into view with his grin, holding donuts and coffee, and she would offer to be his sex slave forever.

"Nicole? Is that you?"

Shit. Suzanne. Nicole whipped around and lifted a foot to race back up the stairs, only she tripped on an edge of the blanket and ended up facedown on the stairs.

"Honey, you okay?" Suzanne came into view holding some sort of brass frame. At the sight of Nicole sprawled in her blanket, with her naked arms and shoulders peeking out, she stopped short.

"Don't ask." Nicole managed to sit up.

Holding the back end of the frame, Taylor came up behind Suzanne. "Rough night?"

Nicole tugged her blanket closer and remained silent.

"Hmm." From Taylor, that was a loaded *hmm.* "Tell you what, let's skip you for a moment and get right to me. I'm selling this antique brass quilt holder today, and I can't be here. Neither can Suzanne. I was hoping you'd be in bed with Ty all day and could handle the transaction for me."

"Ty is gone."

"He's gone out to get you caffeine?"

"He's gone out, all right. *Slunk* out." Nicole scrubbed her face with her hands. "Happy now?"

"Ah. We're back to this being about you."

Nicole dropped her hands and glowered at Taylor. "I'm the one sitting bare-ass naked here."

Taylor sat on the step next to her. "You and Ty do it last night?"

"What does that have to do with anything?"

"Did you?"

"Yes! Okay? Three times! *Now* is my humiliation complete?"

"Did you happen to mention you love him during any of those three times?" Suzanne asked.

Nicole resisted the urge to strangle her. "Why would I do that?"

"Because it's the truth."

Nicole glared at Suzanne, who continued just to look at her serenely. Confidently. Smugly.

"Did you?" Taylor pressed. "Did you tell him?"

"No." Nicole thought about how perfect the night had been, how many times they'd turned to one another, how she'd wondered how that much happiness could fit into her chest. "He didn't say it either."

"Maybe he's just as scared as you," Taylor said very gently, and put her arm around her shoulders. "Love is fairly terrifying."

Nicole looked deep into Taylor's eyes and saw a haunting pain. "You know this for a fact, don't you?"

"Oh, yes."

Suzanne sat on Nicole's other side. "Tell him. See what happens."

Nicole drew a deep breath, but never having been a coward, she stood up. "Yeah. Okay."

"Great, but...honey?" Taylor tugged a little on the blanket. "Much as I think Ty would appreciate what you're *not* wearing, I think you should get dressed first."

NICOLE DID get dressed first, and then drove straight to Ty's house. There was a car parked next to his, and boxes in the driveway.

He was already leaving.

Well, she thought with a deep breath, he'd be taking her heart with him. Chin high, heart hammering, she knocked on his front door. *Tell him*, she coaxed herself. *Just tell him.*

The moment he opened it, she swallowed hard and said, "I love you."

For the longest heartbeat in history, he just stared at her. Then from behind him came a voice. "Ty?" A woman came up behind him, tall and beautiful, with bright blue eyes.

Since no big hole had opened up and swallowed her, Nicole took a step backwards. "I'm sorry."

"No," said the woman. "I'm sorry." She turned to

Ty and smacked him on his arm. "You big lug, why didn't you tell me you had a girlfriend?"

That was it for Nicole, she whirled and ran toward her car, fumbled for her keys, and had just opened the driver's door when she was whipped around.

Ty stood there, his piercing blue eyes narrowed against the sun. He put his big hands on her arms and held her against the car, and when she would have wriggled free, he simply pressed his body in close.

As if he hadn't done the same thing all night long.

She closed her eyes and fought for control. "Please," she whispered, out of breath from the adrenaline and emotions running through her body. "It's been a long, humiliating morning. Just...just let me go."

He was out of breath, too. "Not until you repeat what you just said."

She opened her eyes, but kept her mouth stubbornly shut.

Ty sighed and gentled his hold, sliding his hands up to cup her jaw. "Nicole—"

"I'm late for work."

Still breathing unevenly, he put his forehead to hers. "I shouldn't have left this morning without a note. I realized that after I was halfway home. But I woke up early, and you looked so tired, and...and I needed to think. I went home and there was a message from my sister."

This made her open her eyes. "Did you find her?"

Just like that, Ty's heart tipped on its side. She was shaking, visibly upset, and yet she could put it all away to ask about his sister.

Because she loved him.

It made *him* start shaking. "She found me, that's her in the house."

Nicole looked over at the young woman standing in his doorway with his own see-through blue eyes, his own dark, do-as-it-pleased hair, his own cool, easygoing smile that told the world she was tough-as-hell while on the inside she was terrified.

"Have you talked?" Nicole asked quietly.

"We've started."

"And I interrupted." She winced. "God. I'm sorry, I—"

"My sister and I will have our time." He cupped her face. "But right now it's *our* time. Nicole—"

"The boxes. I...thought you were leaving."

He gave her a half smile. "It sure as hell would be the easy way out, and I like that, believe me. Or I did, until last night."

"What happened last night?"

"I realized I was an idiot." He stroked his thumbs over her jaw. "An idiot who loves you right back, Nicole."

"You..." A half laugh, half sob escaped her. "Really?"

"Oh, darlin', if you only knew how much." He pulled her close. "I thought I enjoyed the wandering, you know?" He buried his face in her hair. "It kept my past off my heels. Moving around, I wasn't just a screw-up, a nobody from nowhere and no one. But then I ended up here, and suddenly there were these strings on my heart." Pulling back, he smiled. "California for one. God, I love it here." He ran a gentle finger down her earlobe. "And then I had a sister who wanted me in her life. That messed with my head for a while."

Nicole smiled. "She's stubborn. Like you."

"Yeah." He stroked a hand down her spine, keeping her tucked close because he couldn't get enough of her. That had given him some bad moments last night, not being able to get enough, which had led to him stupidly getting out of her bed before dawn. He'd convinced himself he shouldn't get used to having her around all the time, because she wouldn't want that. But now he wasn't ever letting go of her again. "And then there's you," he said, kissing her softly. "You, darlin', were the strongest string of all. I'm never cutting you loose. Say that's good for you."

"That's good for me. Really good."

"I want to marry you, Nicole. Have babies with you. I want to start a family and do it right."

She paled a bit, which made him laugh and hug her hard. God, he loved her. "We don't have to start right now. We could just...be. If that's what it takes to make you smile again. Just knowing you love me is good enough."

Her breath caught, and looking uncertain, she bit her lower lip. "What if I never want to get married? What if I never want children...what then?"

"I just want you, Nicole. That's all I need, the rest is a bonus, that's all."

Her smile was slow and brilliant and made his heart tip on its side. "You're my miracle, Ty. Knowing you love me that much."

"That I do, Nicole."

"It's...amazing."

"You don't think you're that lovable?"

"I know I'm not," she said with a laugh. "But I'm selfish enough to marry you anyway." She laughed again, as if shocked by the admission. "I even want to have a little boy who looks just like you."

"A little girl." Ty kissed her, not quite as softly this time. "With eyes just like yours, and a smile that melts me."

"We'll negotiate. How about saying 'I do' on a beach in Mexico? In our bathing suits?"

He tightened his hands on her and put his forehead to hers, overwhelmed and humbled by what she'd given him. "You just don't want to wear a dress."

She narrowed her eyes. "You have a problem with that?"

He grinned and kissed her again. "Nope. But Suzanne and Taylor will. Want to meet my sister? Again?"

"I'd love to meet your sister."

Ty had no more turned toward the front door and waved when Margaret Mary came bouncing out of the house with a hopeful smile on her face. "Is it okay? I didn't mean to upset anyone—"

"You didn't," Ty said, melting Nicole's heart when he reached out for his sister's hand and pulled her closer. "Margaret Mary, this is Nicole. My best friend, my soul mate, my future wife."

Margaret Mary's smile widened in surprise. "Oh my God, really? A sister-in-law? Ty, you're going to give me a sister?" Her eyes dampened and she gathered them both into a bear hug that threatened to choke the life right out of Nicole. "I've always wanted a brother and a sister," she whispered in a voice that brought a lump to Nicole's throat the size of a regulation football.

What could she do? She hugged her back. After a long moment, the three of them held hands and walked toward the house. "Ty?" Nicole asked, watching as he brought their joined hands to his mouth and kissed her fingers.

"We're not going to feel alone, ever again, are we?"

He smiled at her with so much love the lump doubled in size. "Never, darlin'. Never again."

____Epilogue____

Suzanne's Wedding

NICOLE STOOD at the top of the aisle listening to the wedding march begin on the piano. Good God, she was more nervous now than she'd been in her entire life. Her legs were sweating, as Taylor had forced her to put on a pair of pantyhose.

Bridesmaids wear nylons, Taylor'd said smugly.

Nicole had cheated with thigh-high stockings, and planned on getting mileage out of them later with Ty. In fact, she actually wore matching lingerie today, just for him.

Then Suzanne came into view at the back of the church, radiant and beautiful in a white satin wedding dress, her smile filled with warmth and love, directed right at her groom, who stood only a few feet from Nicole.

Ryan—tall, dark and stunning in a tux—had eyes only for Suzanne as well, eyes that looked suspiciously bright.

Nicole met Taylor's gaze. The church was full,

but the music was loud enough that Taylor could whisper without being heard. "This will be you soon enough."

"We're eloping, remember?"

"*Chicken.*"

"At least I can admit love is a good thing to have in my life," Nicole teased.

Taylor's eyes went dark. Haunted.

And Nicole's heart squeezed. Feeling like a jerk, she reached out for Taylor's hand. "Someday I want this to be you too," she whispered.

"Nope." Taylor shuddered. "Singlehood forever. I'll just go it alone."

Alone. Nicole had thought that was the way too, until she'd met Ty. She looked into the pews of the church, and found him.

He was looking right at her, his eyes filled with the heat, the affection, the love that never failed to steal her breath. "Taylor, trust me on this," she whispered. "Someday love is going to sideswipe you out of nowhere and knock you into next week."

"Sounds like a train wreck."

"Feels like one, too." Nicole grinned. "But somehow, it works for me." Ty shot her a slow smile that made her heart do a slow roll in her chest. "Yep, it really works for me."

* * * * *

Be sure to catch
Taylor Wellington's story,
MESSING WITH MAC,
Temptation 918
coming in March 2003.
Return to South Village to see what
happens to Taylor's vow of singlehood!

Turn the page for a sneak preview...

TAYLOR WELLINGTON leaned on the railing, rubbing her temples. She shed her tough guard and half her makeup by swiping beneath her damp eyes. Poor little rich girl, she thought with loathing for this moment of self-pity.

Ex-rich girl.

At the reminder of what awaited her at home—an empty building stripped down to the studs and a stack of bills so high it made her head spin—her eyes filled again.

God, she felt so alone. So damn alone.

"Taylor."

At the low, gruff voice she was beginning to know all too well, she stilled. Thomas "Mac" Mackenzie had a terrible habit of showing up at her most vulnerable moments. "Go away." Instead, she heard his footsteps. Coming closer, damn him. "Mac—"

"You'd like me to vanish, I know. And believe me, I wanted to."

In direct opposition to those words, he came even closer, until he set a lean hip against the railing, facing her, his chest brushing her shoulder.

"I wanted to leave before I even got here," he said.

"So go." She wouldn't look at him, couldn't. No one saw her vulnerable and lived to tell the tale. She didn't care how big he was, how warm—oh, he was so warm. Heat radiated off him, and despite the hot, sticky night, she wanted more of it.

That need alone made her eyes sting all over again. A few of the tears she couldn't blink back slid down her cheek.

"Ah, hell," he muttered. His long hands settled on her bare upper arms as he turned her to face him, and for the life of her, she couldn't look away. "What's going on?" he asked.

What was going on? Only everything.

"Princess?"

Suddenly his pet name for her didn't seem like an insult, not when uttered in that husky, slightly rough voice that was far softer than she imagined he could ever be. Unable to talk without making a bigger fool of herself, she just shook her head.

With the pad of his thumb, he stroked a tear off her cheek. She hadn't worn waterproof mascara, so she probably looked like a raccoon, but even more worrisome than that was the way she reacted to his touch. His thumb continued to make lazy passes over her cheek, his other fingers sank into her hair, and she fought the most insidious need to sob her heart out.

He stood there, silent and strong, not rushing her,

not freaking out because she was crying, not doing anything but waiting patiently for her to pull herself together.

And suddenly she didn't want to pull herself together. She wanted to bury her face against his shoulder and let go. It was humiliating, appalling, and as if he could read her mind, he made a low, soft sound of empathy in his throat that completely undid her. Suddenly her mouth ran away with her good sense and she spilled it all.

"Seeing my mother tonight... You know, my family...we're not close. I don't know really why. Growing up, I was sent to boarding schools. On Grandfather's money. Every few years or so he'd come around and see how his investment was doing, but other than that, we didn't have much contact. I always thought it was because I disappointed him somehow. Or that he didn't have much sentiment in him, but he seemed to enjoy my sisters' company."

"Taylor—"

"No." She didn't want his pity. "You know what? Just forget it."

"You started it, finish it."

It was amazing how private the veranda was considering how many people were just inside. Mac was focused on her and only her. Having that much man, all tall, gorgeous and so focused on her was...well, a fairly intense experience. She'd wanted someone on her side tonight. She'd wanted blind comfort and this man, her virtual opposite, the thorn in her side, was offering it.

No man had ever done such a thing for her. And she could not resist the temptation.

"Mac." Her voice was breathy, the need more obvious than she liked to admit. "There's something else I'd rather finish."

He stood still for a long moment that had her wishing she'd just walked away. Forgotten comfort. Forgotten the wild surging of her pulse that happened every time he was near her. And just when she thought she'd have to take back her words, he simply opened his arms.

She stepped right into them, steeping herself in his heat, inhaling the scent of one-hundred-percent male. He sank his fingers into her hair, lifted her face so he could look at her.

Taylor felt the jolt of his gaze all the way down to her toes. Her problems faded, chased by the awareness and excitement coursing through her. Winding her arms around his neck, she pressed a little closer, absorbing the hoarse sound that rumbled from Mac's chest.

Chest to breast, belly to belly, she stared at him and he stared right back. Her body felt overwhelmed by him, even as she leaned into him. The air crackled, growing more intense by the second in the hot summer night, until she could hardly breathe.

"Is this what you want, Taylor?"

"I want..." *You*, she thought. *I want you.*

Obeying the need and invitation in her breathy voice, he bent his head and kissed her.

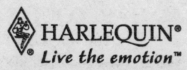

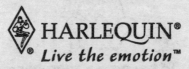

A "Mother of the Year" contest brings
overwhelming response as thousands of women
vie for the luxurious grand prize....

Kate Hoffmann

Jacqueline Diamond

Jill Shalvis

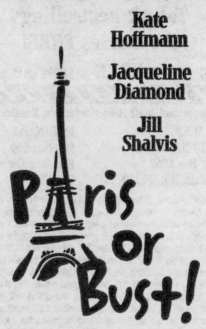

Paris or Bust!

A hilarious and romantic trio of new stories!

With a trip to Paris at stake, these women are
determined to win! But the laughs are many as three of
them discover that being finalists isn't the most
excitement they'll ever have.... Falling in love is!

Available in April 2003.

HARLEQUIN®

Makes any time special®

Visit us at www.eHarlequin.com

PHPOB